MW00781431

WAITING

FOR THE

LONG

NIGHT

MOON

ALSO BY AMANDA PETERS

The Berry Pickers

AMANDA PETERS

WAITING

FOR THE

LONG

NIGHT

MOON

STORIES

CATAPULT  NEW YORK

WAITING FOR THE LONG NIGHT MOON

This is a work of fiction. All of the characters, organizations, and events portrayed in this novel are either products of the author's imagination or are used fictitiously.

First Catapult edition: 2025

Illustrations on chapter openers by Oliver Vaughan.

Grateful acknowledgment for reprinting materials is made to the following:

Epigraph copyright © 2021 by Matthew Salesses, from *Craft in the Real World*. Reprinted by permission of Catapult.

ISBN: 978-1-64622-259-9

Library of Congress Control Number: 2024947761

Jacket design and illustration by Nicole Caputo

Catapult
New York, NY
books.catapult.co

Printed in the United States of America

1 3 5 7 9 10 8 6 4 2

. . . to tell a story is to retell it, and that no
story has behind it an individual.

—MATTHEW SALESSES, *Craft in the Real World*

Wela'lioq to all those who have shared their stories

and planted the seed of imagination.

These are for you.

Msit No'kmaq

Some of these stories deal with issues that may cause grief, sadness, anger and fear. Please take care of yourself as you read. Triggers include racism, missing and murdered Indigenous women and girls, pregnancy loss, murder, physical abuse and drug abuse. While some of these stories are heavy, there are stories of joy as well. I hope you can find a smile in them.

CONTENTS

WAITING

FOR THE

LONG

NIGHT

MOON

(WINTER ARRIVES)

T he pale ones have returned, their skin the dull pink of the early sun on snow. There are more this time, many more. Their clothes are too heavy for the season, thick and rough. Only their faces and hands see the sun. They've been here before and they have departed before. We have watched them, nervous of the cold, not willing to risk the quiet of winter.

Yesterday, after the fish had been set to dry in the sun and when no one would notice my absence, I ran along the river's edge, ducking in and out of the trees so that I could watch them. They don't know we are here, but we know about them. They have been coming here for two seasons now. They arrive in large, strange canoes, but they always leave, some of them die. They cover their dead with earth and wail, scaring some of our smaller children who hear the voices through the trees.

More women arrive this time, and children, some younger than me. The children run around like animals, shouting at each other. Their harsh language is uncomfortable in my ears. Their playful shrieks are louder than the birds that try to steal our fish. Their mothers shout at them, their mouths in constant frowns, their hands raised to wipe the sweat from their brows. The women drag water from the river, the bottom of their dresses wet with mud. The buckets look heavy, bending their backs. They smile very little, these pale ones. I wonder if it is the heavy clothes and stiff shoes that make them bad-tempered.

The men sweat in the sun as they move large stones from the shore and cut the trees from the earth, one by one. The earth on their side of the river is bare now, the stumps from the trees jagged and ugly. Dirt fills the air as they walk; their feet pound the ground in their stiff shoes. With the stones and the trees, they build strange dwellings. There is little sense in their work as it will be difficult to move them to the summer grounds when the seasons change. They have brought a funny thing, not made of trees or stone. It looks like a wilting flower. It sat on the ground for days, the morning dew sliding off the top, running down the side and wetting the ground in a beautiful circle of dark earth. But now it sits high on the top of a special dwelling, hanging in an open space above the entrance. No one lives there, but everyone visits, all of them looking very grim, their heads bent, their eyes on their shoes. When the red-faced man in the black robe pulls the rope, it sings! The sound is steady and beautiful like a drum, only sadder. How can they be so sad with such magic in the air, echoing off the trees, the river, the sky itself?

Father is not worried about the pale-faced. He tells us they will leave.

"They have come before, and they will leave again. When they see their breath on the morning air, they will leave," he explained around the fire last night. I shook my head as I watched the sparks from the fire climb to take their rightful place in the sky.

"But they brought children, they made homes, and brought a magic flower that sings like the drum. Maybe they will stay this time."

"They will not. Each year they come, little one. They come and they leave. They will leave their homes and their wilting flower." Father is sure, but I'm not. I think they may stay.

TINY BIRDS AND TERRORISTS

The last of the night shift has started to fade into the distance; it's time for food and sleep. In the field between us and those dressed for war, a small fire sputters from neglect. We watch the soldiers as they stand in a straight line, blocking the horizon, their face shields hiding their eyes. They shift nervously and look behind them every few minutes. The morning passes this way, their unease sinking into our songs and breaking the rhythm of our chants. We stand, side by side, our arms wrapped around each other's waists, singing and praying. Then, just before noon, as we spread food out on blankets in preparation for lunch, a crack forms in the black wall as they part.

They arrived two days after the television called us terrorists. So many trucks that the ground vibrated under our feet, and the rumbling woke Sisip'jij. Ten or twenty at a time, crawling out of the back of the military vehicles, large tents erected behind them. Two straight black lines, blocking our way to the road, our access to showers and food. They stand so still, watching us from behind their tinted visors, their hands resting on their batons, ready for a fight that we don't want. They outnumber us three to one. They carry guns and tasers, we carry drums and songs.

"Something's wrong."

Mala stands and offers her hand to help me up. Sisip'jij, strapped securely to my back on her cradleboard, sleeps through the tension. Mala helps me to my feet just as the nesting birds lift out of the grass, their bodies moving together, a cloud of birdsong hanging overhead before they bear left, escaping. Opposite us, a few of the men hang their heads. Their chins brush the thick plastic of their chest protectors until the one in charge yells and they snap their heads back into place. Mala lets go of my hand, breaks away from our group and moves to the centre of the field.

"I need to get a closer look," she whisper-shouts back to us.

I'm very aware that I have Mala's baby strapped to my back, the ties criss-crossed over my shoulders and across my chest. The others behind me stop eating and stand, walking toward Mala. The air is breathless in the warm spring morning. Sisip'jij jolts awake and begins to cry, frightening those on both sides of the divide, scaring the last of the birds out of the grass. One of the soldiers thrusts his hand up into the air, his black arm silhouetted against the calm prairie sky. When he drops it again, the air is filled with the sound of rushing water. The whoosh of the water cannon drowns out the sound of the crying baby.

"YOU'RE GOING BACK TO SCHOOL," my mother said over supper.

"No."

"Yes."

"No. Jesus, give me time."

My fork fell onto the table and clanged against the plate.

"You're acting like you have a choice here. I'm still your mother and if you want a place to live and food on your plate, you're going back to school." She paused to take a drag off the cigarette that hung from the corner of her mouth. "And I'm well aware of how long it's been. I loved her too."

I ignored her last remark.

"You didn't finish school."

"Yeah, and look what good it did me. Pumping gas and selling lotto tickets. Nothing spells success like the smell of gas on your hands at the end of the day."

"I'm not going back."

"Fine. Become a rez bum. But you're not doing it here."

She blew a smoke ring into the space between us. I started smoking when I was twelve in a desperate attempt to be cool, stealing crushed butts out of the ashtray before graduating to stealing them from her purse. I quit three years later, the day I found out I was pregnant.

"That's gross, you know." I pushed my chair away from the table. A glass of water sloshed but didn't spill. I retreated to the couch and hid away under a blanket. She didn't say anything when I turned on the television and increased the volume to an obnoxious level, drowning out the sound of her exasperated sighs.

I didn't go back to school and she didn't kick me out. But three months later, just after a night shift at the same gas station where my mother worked, and on the first warm day in May, my grandfather showed up at the front door of our house. I was tired and ready for bed, but he stood on the doorstep, arms folded across his chest, his lips turned down, his cheeks carved out of the earth. I stopped, looked at him, sighed heavily with defeat and got into the passenger side of his truck. My mother had called in the big guns.

"You're grieving, and I get that." He closed the door and started the truck. An old blue Ford, rust creeping in around all the edges, the wooden panels on the back bent with age and weather. "But your mother is grieving and I'm grieving, and you can't just be an ass about it." He flung his arm over the seat, twisting to see out the dirty window as we backed out of the driveway and headed down the road toward the highway.

"You allowed to call me an ass?" I rolled down the window.

"When you're being an ass I am."

"I'm sixteen. And your granddaughter."

"From my experience, that's the perfect age for being an ass. And I know you're my granddaughter. Why you think I'm here? I also know that you're grieving."

We drove on in silence until he turned right instead of left, down an old logging road instead of toward his house or town. I assumed he was taking me for breakfast. He used his thumb to point into the back of the truck where two backpacks sat, stuffed to the top.

"We're going to do some grieving together, you and me. Let the trees hear you wail, let the river sweep it away, let the tree moss absorb it all."

I snickered. "You goin' out for a Hollywood medicine man?"

I do this to people. Say hurtful things.

"See?"

"See what?"

"You're being an ass. We're gonna grieve together and work on that for a while."

The logging road ended, a line of trees marking the line between everything behind and the dark unknown ahead.

"You know where you are, old man?"

"I do, and I also know that I could leave you here and you'd have more of a chance of getting eaten by a bear than being able to take care of yourself. Think about that when you think you're being smart." He grabbed one of the backpacks and nodded toward the other. It was heavy but manageable, covered in a plastic garbage bag to keep the wet out.

Packs on and shoes already stained by mud, he parted the branches and the sunlight disappeared behind a thick wall of pine needles and brush.

"I know what you're doing," he said, turning toward me, only a few feet into the woods.

I stayed quiet, his face a few feet from mine.

"I'm following you through the woods."

He ignored me and stepped closer. I could see the brown edges of his ancient teeth, the smell of coffee with canned milk on his breath.

"You're letting your grief ruin you from the inside out." He turned and walked farther into the trees. "A few tears and quitting life ain't going to cut it. You need to grieve properly. Get it out of your system before it turns you all black and gunky inside."

"How exactly does a person grieve properly?" I stumbled on a tree root and caught myself with the help of a branch. He bent down to pick up a felled tree, a thin birch. Snapping off the top, he handed it to me. I took it and used it as a walking stick, seeking out rocks and anything else the forest could use to trip me.

"It's different for everyone, but you're not going to find it moping around your mother's house, causing her more grief. Don't forget that you're her baby girl." He stopped and bent to grab the bottom of a tall green plant. He dug around the base with his knife until he could pull the roots out of the ground. "Your little one is gone now, but she had a purpose. I know she did. We all do. No matter if we live two days or two hundred years." He dusted them off and held them to his nose, taking a deep breath.

"What purpose?"

"Well, I don't know. You're her mother. Guess that's for you to find out."

"But I'm not her mother. She's dead."

I could still smell her breath. They let me hold her, her tiny limbs taped to boards that looked like Popsicle sticks, needles and tubes everywhere. They let me put her against my chest and sing to her and I remember the smell of her breath, sweet but sour.

"Your baby girl, bless her tiny heart, wasn't meant for this nonsense world. She just knew better. She wasn't ready. It's your job to make it better so, next time, she's ready." He lifted the plastic bag and shoved the roots into the top of my backpack before he bent down and kissed my forehead. "And you're not going to do that working at that gas station and watching *Judge Judy* all day."

I'm the kind of person who would rather curse and say hurtful things I don't mean than admit I could be wrong. He knew this about me and stood waiting for me to say something we both knew I'd regret. Instead, and much to our surprise, I pushed past him and walked deeper into the woods, following the sounds of the river.

When we got to the water's edge, we stopped to set up a small fishing weir, tall, sturdy sticks stuck in the mud between the rocks, obstructing the route of unsuspecting trout.

"We'll stay here a bit and wait. You can listen to your thoughts better out here than you can when watching that television all day and all night. These sounds heal a broken heart." He spread his arms, sweeping them through the air. "I think they have some new fancy word for it now, *forest bathing*." He shook his head and laughed.

"If you say so." I took the garbage bag from the top of my pack and placed it on the ground to sit on.

"I do say so. I just did." He leaned against a large rock that sat on the edge of the water. We sat there, together but apart, looking out over the tiny rapids, trying to see between the trees on the other side of the river. The quiet sounds of the woods softly lulled me into my thoughts, my memories. I looked down at my hand and remembered how bruised it had been from where they placed the IV. I can see her tiny body, purple and red, and the bracelet around her wrist telling the world that she was mine, that I had created something so incredible. But when the weir shook and my grandfather shouted out, the memory disappeared.

"Got one!" He pushed himself off the rock and into the water. He grabbed the fish with his hands, pinning it to the ground before hitting it over the head with a stone. He handed me the dead fish as he dismantled the weir, throwing the sticks into the brush.

That night, he roasted the roots and the fish over a fire, and we drank water, cold and crisp, right from the river before boiling the rest to make tea.

The evening was mostly quiet. I stared into the fire while Grandfather carved a stick he'd found for me earlier that day. He admired the stars peeking through the tree branches as he told stories. A tale about my grandmother, who died in a car accident when I was two, about how he'd come to this very wood and stayed for more than a week.

"What are we doing tomorrow?" I asked.

"We're gonna find your grief so we can look it in the eye."

I sniffed mockingly, but he ignored me.

I don't remember falling asleep, my sleeping bag tucked tight around my chin, keeping the warmth in and the chill out. I slept soundly, the deep sleep that comes with fresh air and exhaustion. The next morning, when I finally woke up, he already had the fire going. A pot hung over the flames, the smell of oatmeal on the chilly morning air.

"I got some breakfast here," he said.

I sat up, shivering, as he handed me a bowl.

"I put some jam on it to sweeten it up for you."

"Thanks." I took the spoon and stirred in the lumpy red berries, enjoying the heavy comfort that oatmeal brings.

"How long are we staying in the woods?" As the oatmeal warmed my belly, I grabbed my walking stick to inspect it. The end was whittled into a point with animals crudely carved into the wood: the rough edges of turtle shells, the wide eyes of the owl and the long slither of a snake.

"As long as it takes." He smiled as my fingers traced the jagged outline of a bird. "Let's go."

I grabbed my pack, slung it over my shoulder and followed.

The sun is harder to track when the trees hide it, and I had no way of telling time. But as we walked deeper into the woods, time seemed to matter less. My grandfather stopped to gather a few mushrooms, dig some early spring roots, bitter but food. I dug around in my pack and found beef jerky and Mars bars in the bottom.

"Just in case." He shrugged.

As we walked along the edges of a shallow ravine, waiting for the perfect place to cross, I saw something out of the corner of my eye—a flash of blue in the dim light of all the browns and greens. I left the path my grandfather had laid out, using my walking stick to keep my balance over the uneven ground, stones hidden by slippery moss. He stopped and turned back to follow me.

On the ground, under the outstretched arms of an oak tree, was a small bird's nest. There were two light-coloured blue eggs, one with its shell broken and empty, the other cracked but intact. I bent down and took the cracked one in my hand, turning it over, inspecting the crack, the lightness of it telling me that nothing lived inside.

"Jipjawej. Robin red breast. Must have been knocked out of the tree." He looked up at the branches over our head.

Something about the lightness of the egg broke me. I could feel it in my chest, sharp and painful. It moved into my belly and I fell to the ground, struggling to get the pack off me. I couldn't get enough air into my lungs. As I gasped, my eyes filled with tiny dots, black and inky. I could hear him saying something, but he sounded so far away. A voice heard through a thousand miles of water. Then the crack in my chest broke, sending the pain up my throat and out of my mouth. I screamed and wailed so that the trees shook and the sky could hear me. The force of my grief pushed me backwards and I lay on the ground. The blue of the sky tried to break through the forest canopy and the leaves rustled, attempting to soften the sounds of my loss. My lungs seemed small and my body heaved as I remembered how light she felt after that last breath, how tiny she was but how the sadness she left was so incredibly heavy. I could feel his hands on my shoulders as he lifted me up, sat behind me and wrapped his arms around me.

"There it is. There it is," he whispered over my sobs. "Let it go."

TWO YEARS AND A BIT LATER, my diploma tied with a little blue ribbon sat on top of the fridge with all the other papers no one knew what to do with. Old bills, paid, flyers and coupons. My grandfather, quietly in his sleep, had slipped away to hug his wife and cradle my baby girl, and my mother was promoted to manager. Nothing held me down, but nothing lifted me up either. Until, one very unremarkable afternoon, I saw it, a post on Facebook from a friend of a friend. I had to be at work in an hour, and I was sitting at the table, sipping tea, fiddling with my phone, my thumb swiping in automatic boredom. And there it was: SMALL BAND OF INDIGENOUS WATER KEEPERS GATHER TO PROTECT THE RIVER, with a photo of a small group of people standing tall, their arms entwined, crafting a human braid. The warrior flag flew behind them, along with the flags of nations older than this one but none of them taught in school. Signs, the words crudely painted on old plywood or bent, torn and water-weathered bristol board: *Water for our grandchildren* and *You cannot drink money*. Behind them, the glimmering thin line of a river snaked through the flat land. I sat up in my chair, nearly knocking the tea off the edge of the table, and leaned over the screen, using my fingers to enlarge it.

I said out loud to no one, "There's not enough of them." I zoomed in on the belly of a very pregnant woman. "And what the hell is she doing there?"

I put remarkably little thought into my decision to join them. How little I considered anything beyond the need to be there, to hold a sign, to stand with them, a small but present strand in their human braid. I packed my bag, threw in some clothes and a few books, a flashlight from the junk drawer. I grabbed the old tent my mother and I had used once, years ago, when we went on our one and only camping trip together. I dusted it off and threw it in the back of the truck my grandfather had left me. I ran back inside to retrieve a small cardboard box, decorated with holly berries and painted golden bells, a dollar store purchase from two Christmases ago. Inside, a tiny blue eggshell wrapped in paper towel. I stopped by the gas station, told my mother to give my shifts away and stocked up. Mom didn't even argue.

I arrived at the camp the day Mala had her baby, in the middle of the afternoon, the clouds grey and wispy. I slammed the door of the truck to the godawful sound of a woman stretching and tearing, just as the little one burst into the world. That night, my body aching from days of driving, sleeping in the cab of the truck and the chilly prairie evening, I used the moon as a guide and set up. My tent was next to Mala's, making me an auntie the moment I drove the first tent peg into the ground. Hard to believe that was only a few weeks ago.

"You're up early, little one. So early that the moon hasn't even gone to bed," I mutter, kissing the top of her head and pointing to the sliver of moon hanging just over the horizon.

The three of us are gathered around the fire. A thin mist hangs over the camp as the sun creeps over the small hills to the east. She looks up at me, her eyes wide, as spit gurgles from the corner of her mouth. Mala has her swaddled, a patchwork blanket of greens, browns and yellows, a complement to the prairie morning. She has the thick black hair of her mother, and the bluest eyes.

"Are you going to give her a name?" I ask. "She's almost a month old."

"Not yet. I'll wait until we're done here, and then head home for a naming." Mala turns her head toward the early chirping of the prairie larks. She closes her eyes, breathing deep. "I love the song of the lark." She pauses. "Reminds me of home."

We watch as one of the birds, its dark horns made of feather and down, flits across the grass until it disappears into a nest.

"You think this will be over soon?" She lifts her shirt to feed the baby.

I shrug.

"Don't you want to go home?"

"Nothing at home for me. And besides, we haven't even started this fight yet." I grin and she lowers her head.

"Tiny Bird. Even the lark is tiny when it's first born."

"What?" I ask, confused.

"That's what I'll call her until she has a name." Mala is looking out across the flat land, pointing each time one of the birds peeks up out of the nest or over the grass.

"Sisip'jij?" I whisper.

She looks at me quizzically.

"Tiny Bird," I answer. "I think. I don't really speak, can only remember the birds." I hold up the language app on my phone, stuck on *tmlwaliknej*. No cell reception on the prairie.

"Crane," I tell her, and she nods as the sun finally breaks through, the mist dispersing. The others will be up soon, crawling out of their tents, wiping the sleep from their eyes.

"Sisip'jij. I like it. Tiny Bird, or Sisip'jij for Auntie." She cradles the infant's head in her hand, bringing her to her lips for a kiss. The baby sighs and yawns.

I fan the flames, getting ready to cook. Our food is in short supply and what we do have is limited to the basics. For groceries and a shower, there's a truck stop forty-five minutes away. We go a few at a time. If they see too many brown faces, they get twitchy. A dollar a shower and the basics: bacon, eggs, white bread on sale, apples. Tobacco: packs for smoking and loose for ceremony, water by the jug.

"We could save fifty cents if we showered together." Evan winks at me. He's been trying to get into my tent since the day I got here.

"In your dreams." I snatch one of the little towels out of his hand and head for the women's shower.

"If you only knew."

"Stop being a creep," I say with a laugh. He's a year younger than me, and he's Mala's cousin, sent by the family back home to make sure she was okay, but he has become one of the most dedicated to the cause in the process. I admire his commitment. It's new and exciting, and he's filled with hope and bluster.

"Only Mala would leave home at eight and a half months

pregnant to go live in a field." He casts his handsome but boyish smile at her. She returns it with the middle finger and a smirk.

That day, we have our last warm shower, our last trip for supplies. When the media finds out what we are doing, we will become willing prisoners, trapped between the river we are here to protect and the men and women hell-bent on removing us.

My grandfather's old truck kicks up dust as we head back to the camp that afternoon. It hasn't rained in days. As we crawl out of the truck, smelling of Irish Spring and carrying bags of food, a man and woman in a tent on the other side of the fire hold up a newspaper they picked up when they went driving, looking for unmanned fruit and vegetable stands. A local newspaper, without visiting or talking to any of us, has decided that we're a *ragged band of eco-terrorists determined to halt progress.*

"What the hell is an eco-terrorist?" I ask, taking the newspaper and reading the rest of the article.

"A word the white folks made up to make people afraid of us," Mala responds.

"People like us?"

"People who know we need the earth more than it needs us."

"Yes, O wise one." Evan puts his hands together in mock

prayer, bowing to her. She ignores him. I can't help but smile. In that moment, she reminds me of my grandfather.

Once we become terrorists, all sorts of folks start driving by, slowing down to take a look, some to help and others to hurl insults. One brazen idiot, at 3 a.m. on a moonless night, throws a rag soaked in gasoline at one of the tents, missing by a good ten feet before screeching off down the dirt road and back into town. Lucky for us, he forgot to light the thing. Others like to stop, speaking in the gentle tones of those who believe they know best, to tell us we aren't accomplishing anything but only making fools of ourselves. We have to learn to live in the twenty-first century, stop getting in the way of progress. Telling us in quiet whispers, as if we won't understand otherwise, that we should go home. A few, modern-day hippies Mala calls them, bring us food and water, stopping to talk, and leave disappointed after we don't want to smoke pot with them and go on a vision quest. When they talk, we nod and mostly ignore them. We know why we're here and if they could only understand, they would join us. I don't feel bad watching them leave.

"These white people think all we do is sit around the fire and have visions," Evan observes with a sniff, tipping a cup of water down his throat.

"Be nice, asshat. They brought you that water you're drinking." Mala points to his empty cup. "Besides, do *you* even know why you're here?"

"To save the water," he answers quickly.

"That's it. To save the water. Nothing bigger than that?" Mala asks.

"Nope, I'm a simple guy. People need water, some people want to poison it so we can't drink it. I want to be able to have a drink of water on a hot day." He shrugs. "What about you?"

"I need to make a better place for *her*." She nods her head toward Sisip'jij, who is sleeping on her cradleboard between us, wrapped up in blankets.

"And you?" He turns toward me as he bites into an apple, a little bit of the juice dripping down his chin.

"I guess I'm still grieving."

"Grieving?" he asks.

"Yup, grieving."

Mala reaches across the baby and places her hand on top of mine.

"I'm trying to get rid of what's left of it. When we win this, she'll know that we're ready for her."

"Who's *she*?" he asks, and Mala shakes her head until he moves the conversation to the woman sitting next to me.

Sisip'jij whimpers in her sleep. I reach over, untie the straps and take her into my arms. She doesn't wake, just stretches, her eyelids fluttering with infant dreams. She smells of campfire when I kiss the top of her head and whisper in her tiny pink ears.

"She wasn't as strong as you are. She was a Tiny Bird with no wings."

Mala smiles across the fire as Evan moves from protector to protector, asking questions and laughing with each.

A couple of days later, a bigger newspaper picks up the article from the local newspaper that labelled us eco-terrorists, which gets the attention of the television news. And that's when we become bona fide terrorists, without a single person asking why we are doing what we are doing. And then the men and women dressed for war arrive.

"Funny, I don't feel like a terrorist," I say as Mala and I sit on the ground, the river behind us, the long prairie road on the hill in front of us. The black silhouettes wander up and down the road, stopping occasionally to look down at us.

"Your brown face makes you one," Mala points out.

The couple in the tent next to mine, their faces not so dark, their English clipped and precise, are interviewed for an article in the same newspaper just two days later. "Protesters" is the label given to their skin.

The baby stirs in my arms and lets out a cry.

"You're strong, you are. A rebellion stirring in that belly," I say, rubbing Sisip'jij's stomach as she cries, gas bubbles moving under my hands. I take a foot in each hand, cycling her legs until the gas releases itself and she quiets.

"Seems like overkill," I whisper to Mala as we watch them mill about, the machines they brought silhouetted against the prairie sky. Sisip'jij's sleeping face peeks over her mother's shoulder. Her eyelids are a light purple, the same as my little one's.

"Trying to scare us home. Now that we're terrorists, they're afraid of us." She laughs. "But they're about as stupid as they come. Them showing up is just gonna cause more people to join us. Talk about cutting off your nose to spite your face." She shakes her head and chuckles.

We turn and head back to the fire, Sisip'jij still asleep on Mala's back, a small white cloth covering her newborn head, when a voice disrupts the quiet.

"You, at the camp," the voice booms over the prairie.

The larks rise, chirping, moving as one across the sky, a dark cloud of irritation. For a moment, everyone watches until Sisip'jij begins to wail.

"You need to vacate this land. This is government land. Go home."

Everyone winces when the megaphone feedback squeals, cutting off the faceless voice.

"You go home!" Evan walks toward us, yelling and battling the baby for airtime. "Or take off those ridiculous outfits and join us. It's your water too, asshole."

Our small crowd cheers.

"No one wants anyone hurt here."

"Then don't hurt anyone!" I yell. Another round of cheers.

"We need you to leave peacefully. This is for your own good," hollers the megaphone.

"When has anything the government has done been for *our* good?" someone from the back hollers. Another cheer as fists punch the air. The megaphone is quiet as the larks begin to settle back into the grass. Sisip'jij quiets too.

"We're not going anywhere until we know that river is safe," Mala yells into the silence, but there is no reply.

Now news cameras are filming everything we do, watching and recording as our little camp gets bigger, pointing at us, broadcasting to the world that we intend to stay. As Mala predicted, more people begin to arrive. Those who join park on the side of the road a mile down, walking through the grass, their tents and food strapped to their backs. In two days, while those dressed in black watch and the cameras film, we go from sixty-three people to over three hundred. Tents circle fires, bannock is handed around, tobacco offered, and there are so many ancient languages my head is humming. Someone's set up a canvas teepee for ceremonies while others head to the river to bathe. Only those who got here early, before we were labelled as terrorists, have cars at the camp. They are useless except as temporary shelter; we can't go anywhere even if we wanted to. The people who arrive without tents sleep in the back seats or in the back of trucks under the stars. Some stay outside the camp, walking along the river for miles to bring us news and food. We steal Wi-Fi from the media crews to read the hateful things being said about us. In the mornings, we wake to new and different signs, hand-painted and tied to posts hammered into the ground. The men in black become permanent fixtures, so we take turns working day shifts and night shifts, standing against them, even when we can't see them in the dark. Everyone still comes to our fire, the original terrorist the first to be photographed, our faces plastered all over the news, unwitting spokespeople.

Each morning, Evan hands out instructions: caring for the makeshift toilets, filling in the used holes and digging new ones, gathering water from the river, boiling it for drink, sending people to the line. Building shelter out of old cloth, ripped tents and in some cases the flags we fly. In the organized chaos, kinships are born.

"I'll take the front line today," Mala says, taking the baby from my arms. "Tiny Bird, Auntie and I."

"I guess I'm on the front line today." I drink the sludge at the bottom of the coffee cup and pass it to Evan, who refills it for himself.

At the front line, we stop to talk to the others, finding a space to lay down a blanket to sit on. I use a plastic bag under the blanket to keep it dry for Mala and the baby. We sit or stand, blocking the way to the river. Sisip'jij is passed around, wrapped warmly and loved unimaginably. Her cries are seldom, but when the drum starts, she wails.

The rhythmic beat of the drum that startles her awake also lulls her to sleep.

"SMELLS LIKE BREAKFAST, wc should grab some." Evan slips his arm out from under my head and crawls out of the tent, pulling his boots on and unzipping the door at the same time. The damp of the night is still on my clothes. Evan moved in two days ago to make room for others as they arrived. I tried to protest, but my arguments were weak, thin and short. Not really a protest at all. He is kind and handsome, and carries the best parts of Mala, kin to Tiny Bird. I follow him out of the tent, stretching.

"How'd you get that?" The bacon hisses in a cast iron pan over the fire. There are more fires now, enough to warm and feed those who join us each day.

"A few of the military guys let someone sneak it to us last night."

An older man, someone I don't know yet, uses a fork to turn the strips of bacon, cracking an egg into the pan, held up by nothing more than an old grate someone found in the back of a trunk. More people begin to gather around, a communal cup of strong coffee is passed around and refilled. I sit on the damp grass. It rained last night. I could hear it beating off the side of my tent, drowning out the songs of the night shift.

The bacon and fried eggs are scooped out onto a tin plate and passed around. Using our fingers as forks, we take enough to get us through, saving the last of it for Mala. She walks toward the circle, Tiny Bird wrapped around her, nestled against her chest. One of the younger men stands to let her have the seat beside me. I hold the plate while she picks at it, her daughter at her breast.

"So, what's today's plan?" Mala asks while dangling a stringy piece of bacon above her head like a noodle.

"Maybe you could rest here, make sure the fire keeps going, prepare the food?" Evan winces as he says it, as he does every morning, hoping Mala will agree. Mala drops her head, chews and glares until he shrugs, waiting for someone else to take the lead.

"He just wants what's best for you and Sisip'jij. To keep you safe," I lean over and whisper.

"My grandmother, English right from England, though no one talks about it—you know, embarrassing these days to have a white person in your family tree—well, she used to say all the time that the road to hell is paved with good intentions," she whispers back, before slopping up the last of the runny fried egg and plopping it in her mouth.

Evan shrugs and moves on to a conversation with one of the new guys.

Today's plan is pretty much like the one yesterday and the day before that: stand or sit in a line, fixed to the earth, blocking their way.

"It's weird that they haven't really done anything to move us out of here," I say.

"It's PR," says Mala, moving into a cross-legged position and settling Sisip'jij. "Men in black, guns strapped to their hips. Bringing those machines here."

The giant machines, dropped off by tractor-trailers and sitting idle behind their lines, showed up two days after the men in black. None of us have a clue what they are or what their purpose is, except to intimidate.

"They don't need to be here, right here."

"What do you mean?"

"They don't need to be right here. This pipeline is hundreds of kilometres long. Those machines were brought here to show the outside world that we're holding up progress.

Fuckers." Mala takes a drink from her water bottle, passing it to me. "They're trying to make it look like we're the bad guys. I won't let Tiny Bird be raised in a world where people like that decide what's good and bad."

I nod and think for a minute, waiting for the words to gather in my head.

"My grandfather told me that my little girl wasn't ready yet, that's why she died. She wasn't ready. And it's my job to make sure, the next time her tiny soul comes to me, I've made the world a good place for her." I look down at my hands, the skin rough and far too pink from sun and wind.

"Smart man, your grandfather. Until then, I need you and Tiny Bird needs you. And Evan needs you," she adds with a laugh, instantly lightening the mood.

That night, I dream of water. We'd all gone to bed once the sky started to spit rain, the tapping on the side of my canvas tent singing me to sleep. As my heavy eyes closed, I could hear Mala in the next tent humming to Tiny Bird. In the dream, I am underwater, looking up, pushing my way to the surface. I know I am close because I can see the light from the sun, but each time I think I am about to push through, the surface moves, gets farther away. My lungs burn and my arms grow weaker until I can't push my way to the surface any longer. When I stop and allow myself to simply sink, I hear crying.

I wake, shaking and struggling to breathe, Evan holding on to me.

"It was just a dream. Just a dream. Shhhhh." He holds me the same way my grandfather did in the woods that day, held me close when my grief came rushing out of me like water through a broken dam.

But it was only a dream.

I LOOK TO my right as the strength of the water from the cannon picks Mala up and flings her a few feet from where, just seconds before, she stood on solid ground. She sputters and wipes water from her face as people begin to yell and run. There's a deafening chaos. I'm turning toward her when my foot gets caught in a bird's nest hidden in the grass. A blast of water hits me in the chest as I turn into it, keeping Sisip'jij behind me. I hear the cracking as I fall to the ground, the bone in my shin snapping and breaking through the skin. I scream and roll over, keeping a terrified Sisip'jij out of the gathering mud. I know I can't stand, so I crawl, low to the ground, dragging my leg behind me. The pain is making it difficult to breathe. The water blasts over my head, rushing past me, knocking others to the ground, and the only thing I can think of is Sisip'jij on my back, a target.

"Mala!" I try to yell above the sound of the water. She stood feet from me moments ago, but now I can't find her. The water is dripping into my eyes and people are lying on the ground everywhere, struggling to stand, being forced back down by the steady barrage. Then I see her, lying on her side a few feet away. She is crawling low to the ground, covered in mud.

"Stay there, I'm coming to you," Mala yells. The baby is screaming and I can't go any farther. I feel as if I'm about to pass out, so I lie down, belly to the ground, the baby on my back.

"Holy fuck, your leg." Mala points to my leg and I look down to see it bent, my shin bone protruding through the skin.

"I'm untying the baby and we'll get you out of here," she hollers over the sound of water being used as a weapon.

Evan crawls over to us, his face muddy, his clothes drenched. "I'll get her, you take the baby," he yells.

Mala unstraps the cradleboard, and I can feel Evan grab me under the arms, dragging me away from the violence.

Mala runs, bent at the waist, her back to the cowards, the baby against her chest. She tries to shush her, afraid they'll hear her cries and target them. I scream out, my broken leg bouncing off each bump in the terrain. We're just out of range when I see the night shift running past us, sliding into the line where they'd broken it. Before we get back to the fire, I look behind and see the line whole again. The gate of men closed, the ground sodden. Then I pass out.

The rest of the day, I lie by the fire, in and out of consciousness, refusing to admit how much pain I'm in. No one has medical training and most won't even look at the leg. An older woman I know vaguely brings yarrow tea to relieve the pain. Evan sits by my side, rubbing my hand.

"How'd this happen, anyway?" he asks, holding the cup of tea to my lips.

"I stepped into a bird's nest. I didn't even see it. I just wanted to get Sisip'jij out of there. How is she?"

"She's fine. She got wet, that's all. We need to get you out of here and to a hospital."

"I'm not going anywhere."

"You can't be serious?" Mala sighs. "I think you've proven your point. You need to get that taken care of." She points to the leg sitting awkwardly on the ground, looking as though it isn't even connected to the rest of my body.

"I'm staying."

"Why are you so godawful stubborn? That won't heal right here."

"I'm staying."

"She'd be okay with you getting some help right now," Mala says.

"I don't know what you're talking about."

"Your girl, she knows."

Mala stands up and places a sleeping Sisip'jij on a blanket on the ground beside me. Her tiny lips are closed and her cheeks pink. I can't help myself. I don't want to cry, not in front of her, in front of them. I don't want to cry, but I do, a silent cry, so unlike the wailing in the woods. Evan holds one hand in his, rubbing it, while I trace the jawline of the baby with the other, her soft new skin under my rough and dirty fingers.

The sky is dark before they finally let a medic through the barricade. They want to take me out of the camp, but I refuse, so the paramedic sets my leg in a plastic cast, stitches up the skin where the bone broke through and gives me a pair of rickety crutches, a box of alcohol wipes and a bottle of Tylenol 3.

Evan holds a cup of water while I down four of them. By the time the moon is above us, I am sitting up, my leg resting on a log. People come to visit, offering apples and advice on pain relief. The yarrow woman stops by with more tea. We all stay up that night to keep the fire going, listening for shouts from the night shift or the rush of water, but as the sun creeps above the prairie, the only thing we can hear is the chirping of the larks and the cries of a hungry baby.

"Shhhh, Tiny Bird. It's okay. Mama's here and we're fine." Mala is lying on her side, the baby on a blanket on the ground, sucking on her mother's little finger.

"Can I do anything for you before I head to the line?" she asks, handing me a strip of bacon and a piece of bread, no butter, no jam.

"Yes, you can help me up," I say, reaching for the crutches.

"Auntie?" she says, her head tilted to the side.

"I'm going." I glare back at her until she shakes her head in defeat. "Help me up."

"We could just leave you here and take your crutches," Evan says.

"Yeah, and all I can see is me sitting at the line and her dragging her broken body toward us," Mala huffs, and I nod.

Evan, resigned to my stubbornness, bends down and pulls one of the Sharpies used for making signs out of the inside pocket of his jacket and begins writing on my plastic cast.

The night shift cheer when they see us hobbling across the grass. The men in black shift from foot to foot. A round of hugs from the night shift before I turn so they can see my cast and the word *terrorist* scribbled in black, the dot of the eye a solid black bird taking flight. My crutches under my arms, Evan ready to catch me if I fall and Mala with her baby on her back, we smile as I lift the injured leg and use the crutches to propel myself to the front of the line.

THE GOLDEN CROSS

I slip it under my sleeping place, carefully lifting the upper right-hand corner, the spot farthest away from where my mother sleeps. My fingers are dirty from digging roots, my nails crusted with dark earth. When the hole is big enough, I place it inside and cover it with a jagged flat stone, too brittle for arrows, but perfect for hiding things.

The basket I use for collecting sits empty just outside the door, the ash weave thinned from age. Small bits of stringy wood separate from pieces of tree woven ages ago by my grandmother's hands before she joined her husband in the spirit world. Sometimes I think I can't wait to go to the spirit world and see her lined face and smell her hair, fragrant with the smell of fire and pine. Other times, I know I would miss my father. I think I would miss my mother, but I can't be sure. She is so different from the mother she used to be. She keeps her love close to her, too close for me to feel it. She grieves for her lost son, the boy who now sits around the fire with my grandparents after a sickness that shook his feverish body and turned his skin the colour of ash. Mother wailed and cried until the moon became uncomfortable and slipped behind the trees to escape. We all grieve for him, he was a sweet boy, but she seems to have forgotten about the two children still on this side of the spirit divide. My older brother uses work to keep his mind busy, to keep his distance from the woman who used to cuddle us, used to kiss our heads before bed. He told me once that distance keeps his heart from breaking all the way.

Many of the things my mother used to do have fallen to me. I cook the food and mend the clothes, gather berries and dry the fish in the summer. In the winter, I keep the fire and mend the walls made of birch. I hunt smaller animals when I can, but I leave the big animals to my father. He says it's dangerous for a girl as young as I am. I remind him that my brother had been ten seasons when he went on his first big hunt, and I am twelve seasons now. But he insists that the help I provide my mostly absent mother is too important to be left to her.

Sometimes, I like to watch her sleep. The faint light from the fire hides one side of her face, which gradually disappears into the dark, but the other side looks calm and peaceful. The lines that she carries during the day rest at night, and I can see the mother I used to know.

Dirt from yesterday's work remains at the bottom of my basket. The wild leeks are in season and they're my father's favourite. I've made it my job to find them and dig them out of the earth and make soup. My mother and her friend leave me alone and I get to wander in the woods on my own. Sometimes my father comes with me, but most of the time I'm alone, with only the wind to keep me company. I'm still not allowed to go far. I need to be able to hear my mother when she calls my name. Today, she and her friend are busy, on their knees, their heads hung, eyes focused on the ground, muttering low and quick in the new language he is teaching her. My father and my older brother have gone to find rabbit for our evening meal.

It was just after my brother died that she found Brother Anthony, or he found her. I can't remember how he came to visit here so often. I do know that he wanders through the trees and along the river almost a day's walk from his own home, made of felled trees stripped naked of their bark. He comes all this way to sit with her for hours at a time. He brings with him one of his books, a large one that he uses to teach her his ways and his words. He makes her use a stick to draw letters in the sand. On days when she is sad, she walks to him. My father says to let it be. The grief will pass and she will come back to us.

Unlike my mother, I find my comfort in the silence of the forest floor as my footsteps land softly on fallen pine needles. I like the way the sun sneaks through the high branches, shaping a golden path on the ground. I see a patch of sunlight and the green of leeks rising out of the earth. The pine needles offer a soft resting place for my knees, and I use a small stone to dig around the base of the leek, taking the stalk and gently pulling it from its place. My grandmother's basket isn't half full when I hear my name travelling through the trees. Even from here, protected by the forest, my mother's voice tells me that she knows I have taken it. I pick up the basket and slowly make my way out of the forest. I am in no hurry to face her, no hurry to feel her misplaced anger. I look into my basket to ensure I have enough leeks to flavour the rabbit stew, and step gently onto the path and toward the sound of my name.

I walk out from behind the trees to see her standing, her back hunched over, the beads Brother Anthony gave her clenched in her hands. Her braid has come undone. I will fix it for her around the fire this evening. She sees me and walks in my direction. She takes my shoulders in her hands. When she shakes me, the beads clink together. It's a pretty sound, even if it doesn't belong out here.

"Where is it? What have you done with it?" She looks down at me, the anger turning her brown eyes the colour of fire. She clutches her neck, but I don't answer.

"Where is it?" She lowers her voice. Her hand reaches out to grab my arm and I drop the basket. The leeks I'd so carefully pulled from the earth fall to the ground.

"Where is what?" I try my hardest not to betray myself. My grandmother always told me I had a face that couldn't tell a lie.

"You know what." She reaches up to her neck. The thin chain Brother Anthony gave her is missing its charm. "Where is it?"

"It was the Wiklatmu'j. I saw them."

The flame in her eyes burns into the skin on my face. "There are no little people. Never let Brother Anthony hear you say such ridiculous things." She looks around her.

"It must have been the Wiklatmu'j. Grandmother told me that they love things that shine."

The sting of her hand on my cheek is sudden and feels like a hundred wasps. She walks away and I watch as her shoulders slump, her head falls to her chest. She doesn't want to hit me, but Brother Anthony says it is necessary to make me good.

That evening, before my father has learned of my misbehaviour, my cheek still red and sore, I sneak back to my sleeping place. I look around to make sure Mother isn't close by. I roll back the corner of my grass sleeping mat. The small piece of flint is where I left it, undisturbed. The earth around it is smooth, patted down by my own hands just hours before. Everything looks the same as when I buried it, but when I move the stone, the hole, dug with my smallest finger, is empty.

THREE BILLION HEARTBEATS

There's a time of day when the world is golden. When it's neither light nor dark. This is my favourite time. When it's difficult to know whether it's night or day. When everything is in shadow.

At least, it used to be my favourite.

Now I exist only in the dark.

"Put your feet on the ground, stand still and let yourself feel it."

My mother, her toes beginning to twist with arthritis, stood barefoot in the rain, her face pointed to the sky. The faint lights from our rusting trailer glowed dimly behind her as I walked up the driveway. Behind me, the school bus groaned and retched as it made its way down the road.

"It's cold and yucky." I hated when she made me stand outside in the rain. "I have homework to do."

"Homework can wait. Come and put your feet on the earth." She lowered her face to look at me and hitched her pant legs up over her lumpy knees. "This is how we're meant to walk the earth. Those shoes of yours are keeping you from understanding."

"Understanding what?" I wiped the rain off my face and spit the cold water to the ground. "Mom, I have homework and I don't feel good."

She waved her hand, dismissing me.

"I ain't givin' up on you yet, girl. You ain't the lost cause they say you are. You belong to the land, you just haven't figured it out yet. It's in your blood, your N-D-A."

"DNA, Mom. D-N-A," I yelled at her as I closed the door behind me. She shrugged, turned her head back to the sky and stuck out her tongue to drink the rain.

Three months later, and less than a week before I left, she wandered into the kitchen. "Hurry up now and finish your food. We're going for a walk."

I was eating leftover tomato soup and macaroni noodles, cold, from the pot.

"What?" The hangover from the end-of-summer party in the bush was pounding my temples, my knuckles sore from punching Eli when he tried to get with me, hitting his stupid belt buckle instead of where I was aiming. He laughed until Regeena laid him out on his back.

"You and me. We're going to walk in this rain. Feel the cool water run off the tips of that hair and down your back, sing to the clouds. I found us a nice patch of moss to stick our toes in."

She turned and marched down the hall, out of sight. It was harder to argue when I couldn't see her and when my own raised voice rang painfully off the inside of my skull. The bathroom door closed behind her, and the spoonful of noodles I was about to eat sat mid-air.

"Mom, I'm leaving in four days. I have to pack, say goodbye to Regeena. You know."

"No, I don't know. You got four days to say goodbye to Regeena. You're not gonna miss a couple hours to go walking in the rain with your mother. Besides, it'll help with that hangover you're nursing." She walked back into the kitchen, drying her hands with the bathroom towel.

"Mom."

"Don't 'Mom' me. Be ready in five minutes. Nothing wrong with spending a little quality time with your mother before you leave her."

"I'm not leaving, Mom. I'm going to school."

"You're going to a city where the air is made of rot, piss and city stink. Bad for the lungs and the spirit. We're gonna make sure you remember what real air smells like, how it feels in your lungs. Air made by trees and grass."

"I've lived here my whole life. Don't think I could forget if I tried."

She made a hissing sound through her teeth, a scolding. She eyed the macaroni, still mid-air. I let it fall back into the pot, the fork clinking against the side.

"How long are we going?"

"For as long as it takes."

"What does that mean?"

She opened the door and made her way down the stairs, her long grey braid swaying with her lilt, the result of a broken leg that never set right when she was a kid. I groaned as I got to my feet and pulled on a raincoat over my pyjama pants and T-shirt.

At the end of the driveway, we turned right, toward town,

the dirt road muddy underfoot. I slipped and caught myself, feeling the muscles around my abdomen brace themselves. The rain was timid, small drops thrown around by the wind, enough to leave a layer of white on the top of our clothes. Mom whistled to herself as we walked, reached up to wipe the water off the top of her head every couple of minutes.

"People stay indoors in the rain, makes the world outside a bit quieter, a more welcoming place to be. It's a perfect time to be out."

She turned down the path that led to the lake.

THE SADNESS HAD A TERRIBLE way of sneaking up on me. It came with the smell of mould sunk deep into things so you knew it was there by the smell even when you couldn't see it. The shades were drawn against the sun so that the room glowed gold. But not the gold that comes with the sunset, but a gold that reminds people of the smell of mildew and cigarette smoke, the kind from a depressing movie about alcoholics and washed-up country singers. The broken blinds filtered the light. I raised my foot, scrambling the dust, watching as the particles danced in the air then settled back into their gentle float.

"I used to be someone to someone."

My words were heavy on my tongue as I took a drag off the cigarette and rolled over to my side. Logan was at the table, his back to me.

"Don't be getting ideas about being someone."

I was surprised when he responded. I hadn't realized I'd said it out loud. He left the table he'd been working at, sorting the tiny white rocks into baggies. I remembered when he was handsome, before the sight of him made my insides twirl and hiccup, bile burning the back of my throat. He lay down beside me, his dirty boots on the pillow, and lit a cigarette. I watched the smoke rings coming from his mouth dissolve in the air and reached up to put my finger through one.

"Give me your arm," he said, coughing.

"No."

"Give me your fucking arm."

"I won't say anything else. I promise."

I tried to roll off the bed, but he caught me by the arm and pulled me back up, my legs dangling off the edge. I closed my eyes and took a deep breath. I could smell my own flesh burn when he pressed the red tip of the cigarette into the underside of my arm, out of sight. It would be worse if I made a fuss.

When he was satisfied, he kissed the burn and went back to the table. I tried to gather myself, get my body back onto the bed, but I fell off the edge. My hip hit the floor with a thud. I crept back up, over the side, waiting. On any other day, a burn came with a buzz, but not that day. That day there was no reward.

"At least give me some," I whispered, holding my arm out from the rest of my body, giving the pain room. "Just enough to get me through." I could feel the headache creeping in and I started to sob.

"Ain't enough, and you ain't earned it either. Get your shoes on and get in the car."

When the headaches and the tears started, I was of no use to him. On days like that, he dropped me off at the park.

"With your own kind," he snickered. "I'll be back later, and you'd better have your sorry ass right here where I left you." He reached across the front seat and opened the door, shoving me out. I tripped over the curb.

"What time? Where am I supposed to go?" I scratched the inside of my arm, leaning into the car to speak to him.

"I don't fuckin' know, just be here when I get here."

I slammed the door as he sped away, cutting off a cab and scattering people sitting on the curb.

"Asshole," I said aloud to no one.

"Don't think he heard ya."

A man, his skin dark and his hair long, leaned against a tree smoking a joint. I craved the sickening sweet smell. I waited for him to say something else, and when he didn't, I flipped him the bird and stumbled down the sidewalk. Past the trippers and the pregnant ones, past the ones who reeked and the ones who sold the shoes off their feet for a fix. Past the park where I stayed sometimes, a blow job for a tent and a sleeping bag. Before I was like this, this place scared me. I avoided it, stayed close to campus. But then it became the only place where I could find grass, green and alive. It smelled so much like home. Sometimes, when he dropped me there, I'd find a cool piece of ground between the tents and lie there, looking up between the branches, pretending that the city hadn't erased the stars, that the swaying trees were talking to me, telling me stories. Listening to the stories helped, even if I didn't understand them. My mother spoke to trees, I just listened.

"THIS LAND'S BEEN ours since forever," my mom told me as we walked in the woods. "Since before the douchebags came."

It was a word taught to her by my eight-year-old cousin at a party. Everyone sat around the table, dice in the cup, dimes set out like silver, ready to be won or lost.

"Those white folks," my auntie hissed, one of them having stolen her parking space at Walmart earlier that day.

"Douchebags," said Paul, not looking up from his video game, red Kool-Aid staining his upper lip.

"Douchebags," my mother repeated. "Douchebags. Like that stuff you clean your hoo-hoo with." She laughed so hard she had everyone else crying, joy at the new word leaking from their eyes and, in the case of my grandmother, a bladder weakened from birthing eighteen kids.

But that day, with me in the woods, we weren't laughing. My mother stayed quiet and let the rain do the talking, stopping every few minutes to listen to the sounds of water hitting leaves. Or waiting for a fox to scamper off the path and out of our way.

"They think people get lost in the woods, but it ain't true. People get lost in cities," she said as we approached the lakeshore. The water was still, the wind dying down the farther we walked into the woods. The raindrops obscured the sky's reflection. In a month the lake would look like fire, a mirror for dying trees. A loon warbled somewhere in the distance. I searched the surface of the lake until I found the little black head just as it ducked under the water, looking for food.

"I'm not going to get lost, Mom. I have an apartment close to school."

"Your daddy was a city guy. Came home for his brother's wake. He was handsome in his grief, maybe more so because of it. Only time I ever met him. You know why? Know why it's the only time I ever met him?"

She didn't wait for me to respond.

"He got sucked in by the lights and the stink. Some people like the stink. I hope that's not in your A-N-D."

"It's DNA, Mom. *DNA*. Deoxyribonucleic acid."

She shrugged. "You are a woman of the land. A woman of the trees and the lake, you belong to the grass. You'll feel it in your bones someday, in your DNA." She looked at me and I nodded. "But until then I want you, I need you, to promise that you won't forget this."

She sat down on a rock jutting out of the water and took off her shoes and socks. The rain was coming down steadily, playing the leaves and the top of the lake like a piano. She was forty-four when I was born. She'd been told her entire life that her ugly face and feisty nature meant no man would ever want her. I don't think they ever stopped to think that maybe she didn't want them.

"I promise," I whispered, leaning on a tree and taking off my shoes and socks.

She reached over and took my hand and we walked toward the water, the mud squishing in our toes and then the cold water wetting the hems of our jeans. We didn't walk far, just stood there in the rain, our feet in the lake, the rain showering us.

"Good medicine," she whispered.

REMEMBERING AND DAYDREAMING are two different things. I remember how handsome Logan was, and I daydream about how it should have been. The day we met, the café was crowded, more than I imagined it would be that early in the morning. I hadn't slept, the rush of early traffic outside my city apartment waking me with the first blare of a horn. I'd been in the city for two months but just couldn't get used to the noise. When they opened the door, I was waiting, my backpack slung over one shoulder, my textbooks pressing against the clasp, about to break.

"Mornin'," I said to the barista as he opened the door and ushered me in.

"Morning, early riser. What can I get ya?"

I sat in the corner with my Americano steaming up my glasses and watched as people streamed in. There were women in heels and men in workboots, but it was still too early for the high school students and the nannies pushing expensive strollers. I hauled out *University Physics Volume 1* and flipped to the page I had fallen asleep on the night before. It was still damp at the edges from my drool. I started to read where my pencil markings stopped. *#16. Roughly how many heartbeats are there in a lifetime?*

"Can I sit here?"

I jumped, kicking the leg of the table, and my cold coffee slipped over the top of the paper cup. He grabbed a napkin and wiped it up.

"Sorry, I didn't mean to scare you. This is the only seat in the place and I'm waiting for a friend." He smiled and I noticed a thin scar that dissected his bottom lip on the right side, throwing his smile slightly off-kilter. I nodded, pointing to the empty chair.

"Physics, eh?" He took a sip of his French vanilla, which seemed like an odd choice.

"Yup, physics." I looked back down at my book, but I could tell he was looking at me, waiting for conversation.

"I'm gonna buy you another coffee, make up for me spilling yours. Whaddya take?" He stood up and pulled his wallet out of his back pocket.

"Americano. Thank you."

His smile, despite its crookedness, was appealing. His teeth were remarkably white.

"Black, please."

I agreed to meet him later that day for a beer. He was different from the other guys I'd dated, if you can call making out with the guys from high school at bush parties dating. He was the first white guy I dated, too. We didn't have a lot of them hanging around the rez, and the ones that did, Regeena warned me about.

"Too many white men causin' us grief all the time. Stay away from them. Stick to the ones you know. At least when they fuck ya over, you can tell their moms," Regeena said, laughing and falling back on the bed, in dramatic Regeena fashion, handing me the joint on her way down.

So I listened. Regeena knew more about these things than I did. She learned from her older sisters. At least, I thought she knew more than me until she called me a week after I left for school to tell me she was having Steve's baby, the skinny white guy who delivered pizza to the rez.

The bar was just a few blocks from school. It was a little nicer than the one on campus. It had lights hanging from the ceiling and big chairs by a stone fireplace. Chairs that looked comfortable but never were.

"Did you know that if you live to be eighty, your heart will beat over three billion times? Three billion. Fuck, that's a lot of work," I said as I sat down on the stool next to him.

"And good afternoon." He ordered me a Coors Light, same as him.

I didn't like Coors, but I drank it anyway.

That night we got drunk, not fall-on-your-face drunk but a good, happy drunk, and he took his workboots, boots that had never seen a day's work, off at my door. In three weeks, my world shrunk so small I swear I could have shoved it into one of those snow globes my aunt liked to collect. Me and him together, lying on the couch. Shake the snow globe and I might get up and go to class. Shake it again and I might grab some groceries and cook a meal. I was so comfortable I didn't see it coming.

"Here, I got you a little gift." He reached into his sock and pulled out a little baggie.

"No fucking way. I don't do that shit. You want to do that shit, you do that somewhere else." I'd seen it before, of course. There'd been a few kids in high school who everyone knew were meth heads and one teacher who was quietly asked to leave his position when he was caught selling to some seniors and a few parents.

"Just this once, I promise. It'll take the edge off, and maybe we can go to that party you want to go to."

I'd tried to get him to hang out with my friends, the new ones from school, but he always had an excuse. He didn't like it when I went alone. It didn't take long for them to stop asking me to hang out with them at all.

"Just try. Can't say you don't like it if you don't try it." He put it on the table and took an empty coffee mug and crushed it into powder.

"No."

"Stop being a pussy." He took a tiny bit of the crushed crystals and sniffed it. He threw his head back and coughed. "Just once, I promise." He grabbed my hand, holding it a little too tight until the tips of my fingers started to turn purple and pulse.

"Fine." He let go, the blood rushing back into my numb fingers.

If there was one moment in my life I could go back and change, it would be that one.

THERE WAS SOMETHING different in her on the walk home. She seemed lighter now, her crooked walk a little straighter, the tune she whistled a little less mournful. The rain had subsided, becoming more of a mist. She stopped a few times to point out things I didn't know she knew. How to tell the difference between the red berries that taste of mint and the red berries that will make you sick. Which leaves to chew to make a pulp for mosquito bites.

"How do you know all this?"

"Your great-grandmother. She was a healer." I never knew my great-grandmother, she died when I was two. "She taught me, but you always preferred those books to these woods. You wouldn't even dance with me in the rain," she said with a shrug, and I instantly felt the guilt that only a mother can impart on a daughter.

"I'm afraid for you, my sweet girl. Afraid that the city will swallow you and not send you home to me. That those buildings will replace these trees. I'm afraid you won't take time to let the mud squish between your toes. That you will walk on concrete and forget us here."

I stopped to look at her. I was taller, a trait inherited from my unknown father, but I'd never *felt* taller until now. I took her small round face in my palms and leaned down to kiss her cheek, a tear coming to rest on my lower lip.

"You don't need to cry, Mom. I'm going to be fine."

"I'm not crying." She took my hands and placed them at my side.

"Well, raindrops don't taste salty."

"And how would you know, smartass. Someone who refuses to taste the rain." She turned to walk away.

I grabbed her hand and turned her around so she could watch me as I lifted my face to the sky, my tongue out.

"No salt," I said.

She laughed, shaking her head at me.

"I will always come home, to smell the pines and dance in the rain, I promise."

She got onto the tips of her rain-soaked toes, her shoes covered in mud, and kissed my forehead. Four days later, I was on a bus to the city.

IT WAS COLDER than usual, or it could have been just me, coming down. The clinic was just around the corner from the park and the sky looked like rain. Rain was the only season in that city. The headache moved from the front of my head and took over my entire skull. The pain in my stomach reminded me that I hadn't eaten in days. The clinic had Subway gift cards along with the needle. Just outside the door was a pregnant girl, no older than sixteen. She lay on her side, her belly protruding, her hands outstretched. I wondered if she had been going for a needle and a sub and just didn't make it. Saliva dripped from the corner of her mouth and her hand twitched. It had been so long since I'd had a hit, I didn't even care that the sweet girl was suffering. I pulled open the door to the smell of lemon disinfectant.

"There's a pregnant girl just outside, doesn't look so good," I told the receptionist before I gave her my name. She sent one of the nurses outside to check on the girl and I felt good about myself for a couple of minutes.

"Rosemary is on vacation. You'll have to see Ginnie today."

"Ginnie? Is that a human name? Sounds like a horse." I laughed to myself as I slumped into my seat in the waiting room.

"You're new?" I asked when Ginnie called my name and I

followed her behind the curtain. She used a little white dispos-able alcohol wipe to clean the crook of my arm.

"I am. I'm Ginnie." She used her teeth to take the plastic off the top of the needle.

"Ginnie's an interesting name."

She gave me a half smile and lowered her head to focus on my arm. I leaned forward to sniff her hair. It smelled like lav-ender. There was a pinch and an almost instant relief from my headache. We all had to stay a few minutes after the needle, to make sure we didn't seize. I sat back in my chair and let the relief wash over me.

"So, where are you from?" Her voice was soft like a lullaby.

"North."

My throat was dry, and my words sounded as if they'd been scratched by sandpaper. She waved at one of the volunteers, who brought me a glass of water and a couple of cookies, the wafer ones that taste like strawberry and cardboard.

"I'm from the North too. Yellowknife."

"Not that far north. Too cold up there."

"It's not that bad, actually." She turned my arm over to inspect the burn, red and seeping. I tried to pull away, but she held on.

"What brought you to the city?" She took out another swab from under the table.

I sat up and looked over to see a little drawer full of swabs, Band-Aids, gauze and needles.

"Probably not what you think when you look at me now. And you don't have to pretend you care." I slumped back down into my chair, my arm still in her hands.

"I'm just trying to make small talk." Her smile started to curve downward.

"School, that's how I got here. I was gonna be a scientist. I loved the stars and I was good at math. Then I met a guy."

She had a soft touch. I didn't know why I was telling her this. She'd forget me the minute I walked out the door. Another junkie would take my place and then another until the doors closed and locked at the end of the day.

"Have you ever seen the northern lights?" she asked. She took out some gauze and covered the wound, hospital tape holding it in place.

"When I was still living at home with my mother." The words caught in my throat, and she nodded.

"Here, take this." She handed me a few swabs, gauze and some tape.

"Thanks." I didn't know what to do then. I felt as though I should ask her to go out for a burger, but she looked like a wine person. I bet she'd never even seen meth. She probably had a dog.

I slumped a bit further in my chair and pushed it back onto two legs, glancing around the loose curtain to see others leaving, pamphlets in hand. From under the table, she brought out a spray bottle, careful to spray every inch, every place where I touched.

"Bitch," I muttered under my breath. I grabbed my purse, shoving the supplies into the very bottom, and yanked the door open so hard it banged against the backstop.

"Wait," she said, but the door closed, cutting her off.

Outside, it was raining.

"Jesus fucking Christ, does it ever stop raining here?" I yelled at no one in particular.

The man with the long black hair was leaning against the lamppost, a cigarette replacing the joint hanging from his lips.

"You a fucking statue or what?"

He shrugged at my outburst.

As I walked, the headache subsided, and the tension and anger began to drain away. I was still hungry, but the sub could wait. I wanted to feel the grass. The cool rain felt good, my bare feet exposed with the cheap flip-flops Logan always bought me. I wanted to take them off and walk through the park, this little piece of green among all the glass buildings reflecting themselves. I wanted to feel the wet grass and the mud. I slipped my shoes off and left them on the sidewalk. I wandered between the tents, listening to people crying, snoring and making love. The sound of cars began to disappear as I lay down in the wet grass and listened for the sound of raindrops on leaves. I closed my eyes and let myself sink into the wet ground. I could feel the rain gently falling on my face and I heard my mother's voice somewhere in the back of my head telling me it was time to go home.

I was pulled up, off the earth, his hands gripping my arm, digging into the burn he'd placed there just a few hours before.

"I told you to be where I put you. Now let's go."

I was unbalanced, trying to stand while he pulled. The pain seared up my shoulder and down to my fingers. My bare feet slipped in the wet grass.

"Let go. I'm not going anywhere with you." I tried to pull away.

"That's what you think."

I dug my feet into the earth, but he was stronger and pulled me behind him. People had started to look out from their tents.

"I'm done. I'm going home." I let my body go limp and fell to the ground. I winced when he wrenched my arm again. "I'm going home. I'm going home."

He turned, pulled me up off the ground and threw me over his shoulder.

"I'm going home. I'm done with this, with you." I tried to hit him, to make him drop me, but I was weak and my fists went limp.

No one stopped him. Not the people watching from the tents or the ones who sat along the sidewalk. No one stopped him when he opened the passenger-side door and threw me in. They just watched.

"I want to go home. You need to find someone else."

"Fuck that. I need the money you bring in. You ain't going nowhere."

"I am. I'll find a way."

He sniffed and I reached up and punched him in the side of the face. Not hard, but enough to make him angry. He turned the car off the main road and we left the city.

The road narrowed and coffee shops and convenience

stores were replaced by tall trees blocking out what little light the sky provided. It's because of the rain that the trees grow like this, so tall and sturdy. A nice person who bought me a meal once told me that trees like the rain.

"Where are we going?" I asked as we moved farther away from the city. "Where are we going?" I said again, fear starting to plant itself in my belly.

I didn't see the separation in the trees, didn't see the entrance to the logging road, but I felt my head slam into the passenger-side window when he made the turn. He braked, leaving the car in the middle of the narrow dirt road. I was rubbing my head where it had connected with the window when he reached across my lap, opened the glove compartment and pulled out a knife.

I remember the first blow, the feeling of the blade slicing through, hitting my rib, and him cursing, as if it was my fault. And the second slicing through my belly, like a warm knife through butter. After that, it all got blurry. I heard the click when he unbuckled me and carried me from the passenger seat into the woods. I should have felt the cold when he laid me down on the wet moss, but I didn't. I should have shivered when he dropped me into the hole and threw wet dirt on my face, but I didn't. Somewhere between the last painful breaths and the last thump of my heart against my chest, the smell of the city dispersed, replaced by the scent of a forest after a rain. I tried to raise my head, but it was too heavy. My hands had forgotten how to work and the blood in my mouth, metallic and thick, wouldn't let me yell. Then the last of the light, seeping through my eyelids, disappeared.

I don't know how long I've been here, the sun warming my bones in short bursts, decided by the wind that moves the branches of the trees. Only the strongest and most persistent rays of light break through, grazing the ground where my bones rest, softening into the brilliant green moss. I don't know if my mother is still alive, if he's still alive, if anyone has even noticed I'm gone. I'm waiting for the moment when this will all go black, when I hit the three-billionth beat. Maybe we stay this way, caught in the middle until that fateful thump. And then we find peace.

I miss my mother. She always found calm when her body was close to the earth, especially in the rain. I wish I could have gone home to her, to walk with her in the rain, to lie with her in the moss.

ANGRY WHITE INDIAN

The place smells like old beer and burnt coffee. A thickness to the air comes with thirty years of cigarette smoke. It clings to the ceiling, the green felt of the pool tables, the posters yellowed with age, advertising beer and baseball. Google Maps is to blame for me being here, at a dingy diner attached to an even dingier motel, eating a tough hamburger and soggy french fries, Molson on tap. It's not exactly the craft-beer type who come here. But it's the only option. It's the only place to eat within twenty-five miles of my meeting tomorrow, and I like to sleep in, so maybe it's a little bit my fault, but I'm going to blame Google Maps anyway. Why are all the reserves so far from civilization? Stupid question, I tell myself. They wanted to hide us away.

The bar stool is wobbly, and when I jumped down to visit the washroom, my feet stuck to the floor. Probably hasn't had a good clean since Christ was a cowboy, I think to myself. Three old men sit at the other end of the bar, the only other people in here on a Tuesday night. I wonder how this place stays open. The bartender can't be a day younger than sixty, but is trying her hardest to prove she's not a day older than thirty. Her eyeliner is thick and it makes her eyes look very small; her nails are long and painted a garish orange. She bends her fingers unnaturally any time she wants to use her hands. But there's something in her laugh that says she was once beautiful and knows it.

Dream catchers hang above the bar, the cheap plastic ones from tourist shops and the airport, with neon fake feathers dangling awkwardly, like they know they don't belong. I wonder if anyone has ever told the people here what a dream catcher is, how they are defeating its very purpose by placing it against a wall. I wonder, but I also know that they probably don't care.

"You hear about those Indians making trouble again, talking about protesting the water again? Fuck, can't they just stay where they belong and be glad our tax dollars take care of them?"

I look down the bar sideways, a limp french fry greasy between my fingers, stuck in mid-air as I try to listen. They look alike, these men. Their height is different, but their white hair, pale skin and pink noses are all the same. Even the way they lean back on their bar stools, one arm draped over the back. They take turns, one leaning forward, the other two leaning back, until a change in conversation precipitates a change in position. But it's the one who I think looks the oldest who's spoken. The other two nod their heads, sucking in air loudly in agreement. The old guy lifts his beer to his mouth, burping as he puts it back down on the bar.

"The other night, one of them was at the liquor store. That young one that worked for Norman for a while and then just quit coming. You remember? Can't hold a job but can buy beer," says the one in the middle with the cowlick. He leans back as if his work is done, his point so righteous that he deserves a rest.

The third, not to be outdone: "Fucking waste of my tax dollars there."

All three nod their heads, the loose skin under their chins swaying with the effort. Cowlick looks at me and tilts his head, chin up, a smirk on his face, a conspirator's grin. He waits for me to nod in agreement.

It's your fault, I tell my mother, *giving me the white genes.* They think they can talk like that around me. If I was brown, they still would have said it, but they'd have said it while leaning on their trucks or at the dinner table around quiet wives and impressionable grandchildren. Not in public.

I call the waitress over, her smile still painted on her face, and ask for my bill, a piece of paper and a pen. She gives me the bill and presses a button and blank paper comes out of the till. She rips it off and hands it to me. I pay and write a note on the blank piece of paper. I head to the door but not before slamming my hastily drafted note in front of the three men. The obnoxious bell above the door rings when I open it and I welcome the smell of fresh spring air. I look back in through the glass door to see them bent over my note.

White people landed here about 413 years ago. Canada is 2,466,614,400 kilometres and the average cost of land per acre is $4,000. You do the math, but I'm pretty sure you're behind on your rent. So pay up or shut the fuck up.

They turn and look out the window as I get in my car. I pull the seat belt and wait for it to click into place before looking at them through the windshield. I put the car in reverse, sticking my middle finger up as I back out of the parking lot.

WAITING FOR THE LONG NIGHT MOON

It's quiet out here except for the sounds we were meant to hear. The wind through the trees sings its songs in the voice of my mother. The roar of summer thunder bouncing off the lake is my father's booming laugh. Only the sound of the coyote causes me to tremble. It's the sound my sister made when they took her words, replacing them with their own. The sounds of my parents are imagined memories, age has robbed me of them, but her cry is cemented in my mind until the day comes when my old ears will hear nothing at all.

Despite the occasional howling of the coyote, I find comfort here in the woods, in my cabin by the lake. I know every rock, every tree root, every path used by the deer, the skunks, even the occasional bear, those animals so familiar to me that they've become my family. A red fox with a missing foot, an unfortunate encounter with a trap, I assume, or a bear with a piece of her ear missing. I know them and I grieve when they stop wandering past my cabin. But still, when the sun comes up in the morning, I wander out to greet those seeking food, or pray for a pleasant slumber for those ready for sleep. I sit, my legs crossed and my back against a big steady tree, my old body resting on the soft moss, and I watch as they pass.

"Good morning," I whisper, seeing the doe approach, her coffee-brown eyes focused on my face. I know this one, she has white hide scattered throughout her brown, her uniqueness a birthmark imparted by nature but a target for hunters. My sister was marked, white skin on her arm colonizing the dark. She covered it with long sleeves, even in summer. I never understood. To my young mind, a birthmark etched on skin the shape of a giant pine would be something to boast of. She told me I would never understand. I was just a boy.

Each time the doe appears, relief washes over me. I always fear she will stop wandering past my door, that the last time she visited will turn out to be my last time with her. A couple of days in a row and I begin to fear she's joined the others who have stopped wandering past my door. I know that my grief for her will be different, darker and heavier. But she always reappears, quietly taking notice of me.

I see her begin to approach and stay still until she's within a few feet. Slowly I raise my hands, and she stops, her long neck extended, her nose high, picking up my scent. We're frozen, living statues locked in a battle of quiet and stillness, until my old arms begin to shake. Comfortable with my weakness, she approaches and sniffs my outstretched hands. Her nose is wet and her scent is musky, like mud after a heavy rain. She never takes her eyes off mine, even when I lower my arms. I feel as if she's looking straight through them to the forest behind me. We stay that way, looking at one another, her nose in my palm, until a pine cone falls, sending her bounding through the trees, and my hands sink into my lap.

MY WEIR HAS A FEW trout this morning. Breakfast will be good. My little cabin has a small garden that gives me most of the food I need. It took time to get anything to grow here, where the trees shield the ground from the sun, but my rows have been planted in between the shadows cast by the tree branches. The garden looks like a labyrinth for small creatures.

The trout will taste good with the wild carrots stored under the floorboards of the cabin to keep them fresh. They're not as sweet as the ones that come from the seeds bought in town, but with a little wild sage, they are tasty. When the food runs low, I force myself to go into town. I am anxious for days before, puttering and mumbling, trying to discover some clever trick that will allow me to stay home. But there is never a clever trick to beat hunger, and I give in to my human need for food and set aside my need for solitude.

I don't like the town. It's loud and full of strangers. But it wasn't always that way. When I was a boy, it was nothing but a wharf and a trading post, small and inconsequential. But then someone found gold and the white people started to arrive to dig the veins out of the earth. I knew some of them, liked some of them. I even attended the school, the stone building with six rooms and a toilet that flushed and faucets that thumped and groaned before spewing water. I wasn't there two full days when one of the teachers used a long measuring stick to lift the skin off my palms. She was angry when she found me turning the faucet off and on, watching the water come from nowhere. I cried when the stick cracked, the whistle of its downward motion broke the air along with my skin. I probably shouldn't have cried. I was nine, after all. But I cried and the boys teased. I couldn't get to my sister; she was on the other side of the building, separated by doors with locks. So my hands bled and blistered, and I cried alone. In the right light, you can still see the white scars where the skin didn't heal properly. A week later, my hands still wrapped, the green infection leaking out around the edges of the torn bandage, I crawled under the broken fence and ran back to the woods.

"You'll stay here with me, work with me. I never thought much of their teachings anyway," my father said as we sat around the fire that night, lit on the edge of the water, the full moon admiring its own reflection. We liked it out here on the water's edge. We liked to watch the winds lift the tiny waves in the summer, capping them with crowns of white foam and quieting them in winter, freezing them solid, mid-peak. Mother washed my hands with lake water boiled over our fire, her delicate fingers gentle and eyes wet while she used a small knife to remove dead skin.

He went for her the next day, to bring my sister home. Instead, my father emerged from the path alone. We never imagined she wouldn't come home, and I never believed that

I would see her only twice more before she was gone for good. Her photo from a local newspaper, saved for me by the first Mr. Johnson, sits tacked above the fireplace in between drying herbs and rabbit furs. The story ripped to pieces and thrown in the fire so many years ago that I can't even remember the season or the phase of the moon when Mr. Johnson read it to me. An obituary, he called it. A recalling of family and friends, of good deeds and sacrifice. It made no mention of me.

DESPITE MY DISLIKE for the town and its lights, hard roads and loud noises, I know I have to go to town for supplies. I'll trade what I have: rabbit furs sewn into mittens, sap from the maples, dried fish. My only consolation is the tea, the one allowance from the strangers that my father permitted to please my mother. The children are friendly enough when they see me. They stare, their curiosity plain on their faces, their questions pointed and honest. The same can't be said for their parents, who tip their hats but look away, refusing to make eye contact. They allow their children the comfort of a story from the *old Indian in the woods* but hurry home as soon as they can. But I try to remember that children haven't grown to hate the things they don't understand, and I forgive them. The parents, I try my best to ignore.

I sometimes miss the winter trip into town, depending on how much snow the clouds decide to send. It can get thick here, and the wind off the lake howls and blows the snow across the flat, frozen water, drifting along the shore. At my age, it's difficult to climb my way out of the woods. When I was younger, it was easier, I could carry things on my back. My back can't do that anymore, it's too old and bent to be useful.

After the howling of a winter storm subsides, I like to wander to the edge of the frozen lake where the blue light of the snow under the moon plays tricks on me. A doe crossing the ice in mid-winter is my sister walking toward me. My cold hands, stained with age and deep lines, reach out for her, but the wind captures her, lifting her into the air in a million pieces of white, whirling upward toward the moon until she is gone. A rock, which has always been a rock and one I know well, is my father, bending, rubbing the ground, looking for tracks. The songs of the winter wind are my mother's words, whistled and hummed from the other side of the lake. Sometimes, when my belly is full of Mr. Johnson's whiskey, I cry out to them, but they never raise their heads or sing my name.

Until this past winter, on a night when the snow had fallen thick and quiet, gently lying on the forest floor. I built myself a small fire by the lakeshore on a night without the howling winds or the violent creaking of the trees. There was no blue snow on this night, only the ghostly light of a clouded moon. I sat, wrapped in hides and furs, my small fire beside me. On one of those nights the doe appeared and whispered from the frozen shore of the lake.

"Brother. When the spring frogs are quiet again and summer has passed, when the harvest is done, but before the long night moon, we will come for you."

I stood, the hides and furs dropping to the ground, and called her name. But the forest swallowed my voice and she turned and ran off into the trees.

"Don't go, please," I cried, but the lake responded only with a crack of the ice.

The next morning, Mr. Johnson's whiskey still swirling in my belly and aching in my head, and absent of the forgetfulness that sometimes comes with the drink, I remembered her. I ran outside as the harshness of daylight stung my eyes, but she wasn't there. Only the memory of her brown eyes and the message she brought.

But it was only this morning, when the patterned doe stopped by my door, her eyes fixated on mine, that I understood the message. Today, as I packed up my sled, my breathing harder and my old heart beating faster than it probably should, I made my peace with her words. It will be good to see her again.

I don't know when they will come for me so have no choice but to go into town, to trade my syrup for some flour and salt. Sell my mushrooms and buy a new bottle of whiskey, *firewater* my mother used to say. "Given to us to ignite an unnatural fire that will burn us off the earth." But sometimes it's good to have a drink, especially when the coyotes howl.

After my breakfast of fresh trout and carrots, grilled over the open fire, I pack the ceramic jars of maple syrup on the small sled. I used to be able to take four, but now my strength allows only two, and even those I can't fill to the top. The sled is easier than the wagon; the wagon doesn't do well over uneven ground. I tie the jars down and head out. The path is narrow and if you're not looking for it, you'd miss it, unless you'd walked it each season for the past eighty-six years. My father built this cabin, when some of the others moved to the reserve. He refused to be confined. He cut the trees, mixed mud and grass to fill the holes, gathered stones for a hearth inside and built a home for us. I wish my sister had understood that this cabin was an act of love and protection, not, as she once insisted, a punishment.

"Far enough away that they won't bother us and close enough if we need something. They don't seem to be going anywhere now, so we just have to get along as best we can." My father slung a log over his shoulder, and I grabbed a few smaller rocks from the shore, collecting them to fill in the holes in the fireplace. The town was only meant to be a camp, temporary while they waited to see if there was enough gold in the ground. And there was gold—enough gold for houses to be built, stores to be stocked and churches and a school to be erected. So they stayed and we retreated, but not my sister.

The day she arrived, standing at the end of the path, I was returning from collecting water and her stillness startled me. She stood, framed by the trees in the semi-darkness that inhabits the woods, as if waiting to be invited into her own home. I hadn't realized until she stood in front of me that her face had been slowly fading from my memory. I couldn't recall the shape of her nose or whether her eyes lifted at the corners when she laughed the way our mother's did or if her lips were wide or narrow. The only thing that ever stayed fixed in my mind was the darkness of her eyes.

And while I had been forgetting, Mother never could. Each season when the warm air faded into cold, she would take a package to the school—new rabbit-fur mittens, dried fish and berry teas. And each spring when the cold lifted, she would go into old Mr. Johnson's store and buy her a new dress, using money she got from making the same rabbit mittens I now make for the young Mr. Johnson. But on this day, when she appeared at the end of the trail, her figure framed by the tall trees and almost unrecognizable as the sister I had left at the school almost a decade ago, she frightened me. She smiled but stayed where she was, silent, a ghost. I called for Mother.

"I'm not staying. The church said that once I am old enough, they will find me a place to stay further south and work until I find a husband. I'm going to live in a city with lots of houses and lots of people." She sat on the floor with us, using her hand to push some dust away from her. She used their words and Father had to translate them for our mother.

"Where are your words?" He stopped her mid-story about a teacher who thought she could find a good husband despite the darkness of her skin.

"I don't use them. They are not my words anymore, they are yours."

My father didn't translate, and my mother looked on anxiously.

My sister didn't stay for dinner, leaving my mother in tears and my father bad-tempered. She walked back down the trail alone. The next time I saw her, it was the picture and the article read to me by the old Mr. Johnson before he gave the store over to his son. He told me that she'd never made it out of this little town but she had indeed found a husband, one who beat her to death when he was unhappy with his dinner. He spent three months in prison and now walked the same roads that I had to venture onto for supplies. I still look down when I walk these hard roads, wondering if my steps have fallen into his. I walk and I curse him. I took the obituary home to my cabin, thankful my mother and father were gone, and tore the edges around the picture until only her face remained, and threw the rest into the fire.

"You could have come home," I whispered as I placed her photo above the stone fireplace, taking a long, fiery swallow of whiskey. "You could have come home." But she hadn't seen me that night, she didn't know I was there to get her. She never knew that I witnessed it, what they did to her. I watched as they turned her soft brown eyes into coal.

THE NIGHT I WENT TO GET HER, to bring her home, the air was cool. I knew how to get in, the same way I had got out and run back to the woods, hands blistered. The fence by the gardens where they grew the food had a hole in it. Nothing had changed in the five years since my escape. Sometimes the foxes got in and took a few chickens and they'd mend the fence, but most of the time it was torn enough to get a small boy through. I was bigger now than when I made my escape, but I was also stronger. My years of helping Father in the woods had made my arms round and strong, strong enough to bend the chicken wire and slide through.

I shimmied under and stopped only once when my sweater got caught on a piece of the fence. I freed myself and walked low across the yard, hoping the chickens would stay roosting and not give me away. The lights were on in the sleeping rooms, but no faces looked out. From where the sun sat, I knew that they were kneeling at the foot of their beds, exhausted, and reciting their prayers.

I could see my breath on the air. I shivered and wrapped my arms around myself, standing against the red brick of the building below the girls' section. I'd have to climb the drain-pipe to peek in the window and hope she saw me before the others did, hope that she recognized the face of her own brother. It had been two years since she'd walked down the trail and away from us. But now, I needed her to come home. Mother, when her fever broke, asked for her, wept her name. The white doctor, the only white man ever in our cabin, called it cancer, something no man or medicine could cure. My father had sent me for her, to bring her home.

"You do know what you did was wrong?" It was the voice of the Father, deep and soft but with a hardness that didn't belong in a school. "Look up from the floor and answer me." His voice didn't waver, but quietly conveyed the anger behind it. There was a sobbing, and I shifted my body along the wall until I was under the window. I turned to stand on my toes, my hands on the outside sill pulling me up. The window was wet with condensation, but the open crack let me see in, and I could feel the heat from the fireplace escaping the room.

"I don't . . . It was an accident." Our accent but their words. Her voice was so low I couldn't be sure it was hers.

"I don't believe in accidents, and neither should you. It's a lazy excuse for bad behaviour." The Father paced in front of her. "You know we don't allow the devil's tongue here." The click of his shoes on the wooden floor stopped. The lanterns were lit, and a fire cast an orange glow on the room. I watched as the teacher, the same one who'd given me my scars, gripped my sister's head and held her mouth open while the Father, so unlike any father I had ever known, stuck a pin, the same kind used by Mother to hold garments together while she sewed, through the tongue of my sister. A howl escaped her. It drifted through the crack in the window and burrowed into my ears, to stay there forever. I gasped and ducked back down under the sill, afraid of being found out. No one came to the window.

"You will not speak that heathen tongue. Do you understand? I won't have you speaking to the young ones like that, telling them devil stories in a devilish tongue. Nod if you understand."

I pulled myself back up in time to see her nod, and he pulled the pin out quickly, throwing it in a basket next to the desk before taking the back of his hand and driving it into the side of her face. She was silent this time, no howl. "You were coming along so well." He sighed and stopped his pacing to stand directly in front of her. "You need to know that we do this out of love, love for your soul." He took her head in his hands, leaning down, her blood slipping into the creases of his hands, between his fingers. "It's not your fault, my dear. Not your fault. But we need to make you right for God."

My sister sat there on her knees, blood dripping off her chin, water coating her eyes. "The eyes of a doe," my mother used to say. "Soft and gentle, but vulnerable to those who feign kindness."

I wanted to climb in the window, to take the safety pin from the basket and shove it into his eyes, to watch him bleed, but I stayed frozen and watched my sister shake her head. Watched her mouth the words, "Yes, Father."

MEMORY IS A STRANGE THING. Now, decades later, I don't remember the face of the Father or the cadence of his voice, I don't remember the journey home without her, I don't remember what I told my father that evening, only that my mother died the next morning. And my father, overcome by grief, didn't have the heart to see to the freedom of my sister. But I remember the colour. The blistering yellow and orange of the fire, the redness of her blood, like a summer sunrise before a storm, the brown of her watery eyes. So different from the newspaper article, her brown eyes obliterated by greyness.

"Mr. Whiteduck!" a small girl cries out when I open the door to the young Mr. Johnson's store.

I'm so lost in my memories that it startles me. It's not often I hear my own name and even less so with such excitement. Mr. Johnson glances up from the ledger he's writing in, a half smile of recognition crossing his face.

"Well, here you are. I was beginning to think you'd died out there in the woods." He lifts the hinged counter that keeps customers on the other side. "What have you got for us today?" He slaps me on the back and looks past me at the sled I've dragged through the woods. Mr. Johnson buys my maple syrup and gives me a deal on seeds and flour, sugar and tea. Sometimes he hangs my mittens in the window for sale, and when I come in the next time around, he hands me money if they sell. I look over to see no mittens in the window, despite having left six pairs the last time I was here.

"I've got some syrup and a few pairs of those mittens."

"People love those mittens. I had a woman come in the other day looking for them since the weather's turning now." He heads back to the counter and ducks under this time. He hands me an envelope. Inside is thirty dollars.

"Your profits."

"That's an awful lot for my mittens, Mr. Johnson. Don't you think?"

"No, I don't. Some people just recognize good craftsmanship." He smiles. "Now let's unload those jars and hang the new mittens. Be gone before the end of the month, I guarantee."

The little girl's been standing there watching, waiting for her turn to interject.

"Are you going to tell us a story, Mr. Whiteduck?"

Her father, the half smile, takes her by the shoulder and whispers for her to leave the old man alone. Mr. Johnson says the children like me because I'm an oddity.

"People just don't live in the woods all alone. They think it's . . . odd, and a little exciting, I suppose. Just pay them no mind. They're just curious about you, that's all."

I didn't understand it then and I guess I still don't. I've been coming here and telling stories since old Mr. Johnson opened this place. Both Mr. Johnsons have been nothing but good to me all these years. Aside from the animals, they would be the closest I have to friends.

He helps me unload the jars and takes the six pairs of mittens I've brought, four brown and two white. The people are standing in line inside, waiting to pay, but he attends to me first. His is the best store in town and he knows they'll wait. We carry the jars inside, and he returns to his customers while I wander up and down the narrow aisles, looking for the items that will get me through the next couple of weeks. I glance among the faces in the store, looking for the one who killed my sister. I've never laid eyes on him, his picture wasn't in the obituary, but I feel in my old bones that I would know him. But none of these men, here with children or picking up supplies for dinner, look capable of such violence. But then again, no one really does.

"The winter moons start soon," I whisper to myself, running the tips of my fingers along the neatly stacked foods. A box of salt, a pound of lard, some smoked bacon and a bar of chocolate for a treat. Red Rose and a bag of sugar. Mr. Johnson gives me a couple of bottles of his cheapest whiskey, pouring them into empty milk jugs so people won't talk. At the front I buy some penny candy, a big paper bag of it. Mr. Johnson pulls a chair up by the window in front of the cleaning supplies and three children stand waiting, their parents patiently lined up behind them.

Transaction done, bartering completed, I sit down in the chair; my joints creak and snap on the way down. Every year I tell the same story, the one with the seven birds who chase the bear across the sky. But this year I pause, and they look at me anxiously.

"Did you ever hear about the young girl who died before she was meant to?"

They all shake their heads no.

"Well, because she died before she was ready, before she was done on the earth, she sent her spirit back from the other side and she placed it in the body of a newborn doe."

Their eyes widen and the one little girl leans forward, her elbows on her knees, chin in her hands.

"The doe inherited the girl's deep-brown eyes and her birthmark, a white one that ran from the inside of her wrist right up to the elbow, shaped like a tall pine tree. The birthmark was so unique that when her spirit entered the doe, it turned her hide white in places. To this day, that doe wanders these woods."

"I've seen that doe," says one of the fathers.

The children gasp and I smile, leaning over to hand out the penny candy. On the other side of the window the sun is sinking, and the clouds are coming in quickly.

"Looks like snow," says Mr. Johnson as he finishes loading my supplies onto the sled. "You sure you have enough here?"

"I've got plenty to get me through the next little while. But thank you, Mr. Johnson, for everything."

He nods his head, slaps me on the shoulder again and goes back inside.

I grab the ropes of my sled and head back toward the woods, passing shop windows preparing for the holiday they call Christmas, past the stores with clothes and pots and pans, past the school. I stop and look. The grey stone is cold. There are no lights on now, no fires blazing. The little girl, the same one whose excitement frightened me earlier, has been walking beside me. Her parents follow close behind. She talks a blue streak, asking why a doe would come back, why would she stay here when she could go anywhere? She tells me about her own birthmark, red and shaped like a strawberry, just under her right arm. I look down and smile at her and she takes my hand in hers, her white rabbit-fur mittens soft to the touch.

We stand that way, so quiet you can almost hear the storm clouds floating by, her parents behind us, waiting.

"It's just a school, Mr. Whiteduck," she says, letting go of my hand. "Merry Christmas and see you next time. Thanks for the candy." She turns, taking the hand of her mother, who nods her head before they all turn and walk in the opposite direction. I can hear the little one chattering all the way to the corner, where they turn and move out of my sight. I wave and turn toward home. I feel the gentle coolness of the first snow on my face as a curtain of green and brown takes me back to the quiet.

THE STORY OF THE CROW
(A RETELLING)

Did you know that the crow was once white? Whiter than fresh snow at noon under a winter sun, whiter than the soft clouds that pass over the tops of trees in summer, whiter than the foam that forms where water meets land. Did you also know that the crow had a beautiful voice? The song of the crow was known the world over. You would always know the song of the crow because its beauty was unmatched even to those unfamiliar with the ways of birds. Hearing the sound of the crow meant good fortune was coming your way. Such was the beauty and the power of the crow's song. And of course the crow was the smartest of the birds. And not only the birds, but the smartest of all the animals. Every animal sought her advice. From where to place their nests, to how much food to store for the winter, to how to fall in love.

The crow would watch over all the animals, those who walked, those who swam, flew and slithered. She would fly silently among the branches of the large maple and giant oak, skimming past the needled firs and the pines, singing her song, and they would call back to her and she would be happy. She would pluck a drowning hummingbird out of a pond or rescue a baby robin redbreast who'd fallen from his nest. Once, it is told among the forest creatures, she saved Muin, the bear, the largest and most powerful of animals, when she got caught up in a dense web of brambles and was unable to free herself. But the crow would never tell these stories, such was her humble nature. She would sit high atop the trees telling the news of the forest and everyone would stop to listen, but not once did she speak of her own remarkableness.

Then one day a rumble of thunder and the crack of lightning echoed throughout the forest. A very small squirrel, his head previously buried in his collection of acorns, organizing them for winter, shot his head into the air, sniffing. He'd heard thunder before and seen the wonders of lightning flash across the sky, but this was different. He sniffed and sniffed, catching the faint trace of smoke on the air. He waited, his ears perked, until he heard the crackle of flame on tree, and then he broke into a run.

The wise crow would know what to do.

The crow, sitting on a branch, her eyes heavy with afternoon sleepiness, saw the squirrel racing toward her, darting through the trees, leaping over roots and stones, chirping frantically.

"It's a fire, wise crow. A fire is coming."

The crow lifted her beak into the air, still and quiet, detecting the smell of smoke. Without a word to the frightened squirrel, the crow began to sing, loudly and with urgency. She opened her beautiful white wings and took flight, singing a song of warning to the animals, her beautiful voice echoing off the trees and waking those who slept, stopping those who worked.

Every animal listened to her song, a song of warning, and followed her through the forest, catching sight of her white body darting in and out of the trees. The crow, being the wisest of the animals in all the forests, led the others to the river and to the other side, where a meadow sat. The smaller animals, the squirrels and rabbits, the martens and the snakes, scampered or slithered across fallen logs. The larger animals, the coyotes and the bears, swam across the quiet waters.

From the safety of the riverbank, the animals watched as the smoke billowed from the trees and the flames licked the sky. They watched as, over and over again, the crow went into the forest deeper and deeper, warning the animals and guiding them out to safety. And never did she stop singing her warning, until the smoke got into her throat and her voice began to change. Each time she emerged from the smoke, her voice was different, the beautiful voice of the crow became rough until it was nothing but a caw. And each time she emerged, the flames staining her beautiful white feathers, she grew darker from the smoke and the soot. But when the fire reached the river and had nowhere else to go, the crow was happy. She emerged from the forest one last time, her voice broken and her body black. To this day, the crow is still the wisest of the animals, her feathers black like midnight with no moon and her voice a caw because she was brave.

LE GRAND DÉRANGEMENT

I lie by the fire, on the other side of the narrow body of water they call *rivière* and we call *sipu*, my hands tucked behind my head, holding the burden of my tiredness. The rest of my family has gone to bed, but something about the absence of the insects keeps me here, tending to a dying fire, suspicious of the quiet. I was following the stars as they danced in their predictable way across the dark sky, waiting for the sun to carry the night away. The fish we caught earlier are drying on the racks and the baskets of plump blackberries shine under the half moon. My youngest daughter picked them today, her tiny fingers still stained with the juice when her mother carried her off to bed.

While I battle both sleep and wakefulness, my nose fills with the scent of burning grass and the snap of fire breaks my semi-slumber. The smell is too strong to be coming from my small spot here near the water's edge. I lift myself and look toward the sound. Across the water, I can see the orange flames as the smoke begins to obscure the moon. I don't hear the yelling right away, just the sound of fire as it spreads, crackles and splits the night. The plants that they grow for food are burning. They don't hunt and fish the way we do, they prefer to stay inside during months when the world is white and cold. I think of Gilbert and worry for him and his daughter.

"Gilbert, let me show you how to hunt rabbit and make warm furs for yourself," I offered my friend just last winter.

"*Non*," he said in his accent brought from across the ocean, "then I wouldn't need to be friends with you." He laughed.

We stood inside his one-room cabin, a quilt drawn at the back where Hélène slept. It's a simple cottage, the large fireplace for cooking and washing, a chair Gilbert crafted himself sitting by the fire. The pillows sewed and stuffed with straw by Hélène. I prefer the floor. Gilbert is one of the few who lets me inside. The others make me wait outside when we trade for food and goods. He offers me tea and I accept. I like the warm bitterness of it. I always take some home to my wife, but she adds the leaves of a berry bush to soften the taste. From behind the curtain, I heard the soft snores of Hélène.

"Don't you find yourself restless in the winter, Gilbert? Don't you long to be outside, to breathe in the cold air?" I asked one evening as we sat in front of the fire.

"I was poor in my homeland, without fire in winter. I had no crops, begged for food. Here I have a home, I have protection from the winter wind, from the air that steals your breath." He nodded toward the fire raging in the large open fireplace. "Here I have my land and a future for Hélène. I will leave the winter air for you, my friend. I will stay inside and count my blessings," he said, chuckling to himself.

We heard Hélène cough a little in her sleep.

"She is smitten." Gilbert bent over his chair and whispered, "A young man named Paul." He nodded his head toward the curtain. "I think she will marry and leave her poor father alone. Then maybe I will go with you into the woods and breathe your cold winter air."

"Je viendrai toujours prendre le thé."

My French has improved these last few months with Gilbert. The others speak to me in lilting French, not allowing me to grasp the fullness of the words, keeping sentences as secrets. But Gilbert speaks to me like an old friend. And now I camp just down the river and on the other side. Tomorrow, I'm planning to take some of the berries to Gilbert and Hélène. A gift in appreciation of his friendship.

My nose and eyes begin to sting with the smoke drifting over the water. It looks like morning fog, but there's so much more of it. My tired legs take me down to the shore. The mud captures my bare feet, pulling me gently into the earth.

"What's happening?" My wife is awake and stands beside me, watching the flames. She grips my hand when we hear the first scream. I've heard their screams before, ones of agony when a finger is lost to the contraptions they use to grow food, ones of pain when their women give birth, ones of joy when the children see the first calves in the spring. I have heard their screams, but none like this. This scream turns the saliva in my mouth sour. And then I hear a gunshot. It's far off and muffled. My heart stops beating, if only for a second. Beside me, my wife jumps.

"Should we do something?" she whispers.

"What can we do? We don't even know what's happening. May just be a fire, and a fire in the grass will have to extinguish itself. There is nothing we can do to stop it. Just be glad we are on this side of the water."

"And the gunshot?" she asks.

"I don't know. I think we need to wait until daylight." I turn to step out of the mud when she lets go of my hand and points into the darkness.

Two lights sway above the water. The moon is too obscured now to help, and the sun won't rise for hours. The lights look like drunk ghosts floating along the top of the water, and my heart moves from my chest to pound in my throat before I hear the sloshing of water against wood. The sound of the boat mingles with the cries of women and children and the soft but firm shushing of men. I turn to take my wife by the hand, but she is already climbing back up to the camp, keeping low on her hands and knees. The mud makes a sucking sound as I heave my feet onto the grass and follow her. When I catch up, she's belly down, her hands holding the grass to the side so she can watch.

"What is it?" she asks, an unfamiliar quiver in her voice.

I crawl over to the fire, using my hand to smash down the last of the wood, separating the last of the flames, and watch them die. "I don't know. Stay quiet." I wipe my hands on the damp grass before sidling up to her.

The two lanterns sway from the bow of an English boat loaded with people, far too many people to be headed out into the bay. Any current or wave carried across the water by a strong wind and they will all be lost. In the dim light I can see them huddled together, some crying, mothers burying the heads of children in their soot-covered aprons, men tied to the railings, their hands above their heads. The English curse and walk back and forth across the deck, the echo of their shoes fighting the fire for attention. I see one of them kick a man. A woman cries out and the same man hits her on the side of the head and she quiets. They are moving slowly, four small dinghies tied to the side, bouncing off the wooden body of the larger vessel. They're almost to us when another boat and then another appear out of the darkness. These are smaller, the men I trade with paddling them toward the bay, their hulls overflowing with women and children, some crying, the babies sleeping, indifferent to the chaos.

The flames are higher now and reflect on the water. Some of the faces scan the shoreline and I struggle with my own conscience. I could stand and ask for an explanation of what I am seeing, but I could also be shot the moment my head appeared above the high grass. And while my French is improving, I don't speak the language of these men. Some of the men I trade with, their faces bloody, their hands swollen, struggle to guide the oars, moving away from their homes and out into the bay. The English scream and point their guns, occasionally firing them into the water to scare the frightened. The shots echo off the cliffs behind me and wake the children. I can hear them shuffling. My wife leaves my side, slinking through the grass to shush them. The boats continue to appear. The boats of the French and the English, overflowing with families, their pale faces scared in the dark. Then I see Hélène.

I scan the faces in the faint light, but I can't find Gilbert. Hélène's boat sways in the wake of the one before her, the lantern casting an eerie glow on her face, blotched red and wet with tears. For a moment I think she looks directly at me, but I know I can't be seen. I look behind me to see the last thin trail of the smoke from my dead fire drifting toward the sky. When I look back, she is standing and the English and French are screaming at her to sit. But rather than sit, she stands and allows herself to fall over the side of the vessel. The dark water opens and welcomes her.

The English fire a few shots into the water, cursing her, and pronounce her drowned. One of the women stands to grab the gun, sending a shot into the air. She is rewarded with the butt of the musket to her face. She falls back into the boat, holding her apron to her split cheek. Hélène hasn't surfaced. Only the movement of the boats disturbs the water.

Behind them, in the darkness and the long grass that grows along the bank, I see Hélène surface. I can see more lanterns approaching, but I'm still too far away for them to notice my movements. I stand, my back bent to the height of the grass, and whisper, "Hélène?" but there is no answer. I move toward where I thought she surfaced, but now I can't be sure. I can't trust my senses in this chaos. The night is cast in shadows, created by the burning fields, making it difficult to know what is real and what is imagined. The crackling of the fire fights with the sound of my voice, but somewhere in front of me I hear, "I'm here." The yellow of her dress helps me to find her, lying on the bank of the river, her hair plastered to one side of her face, the other in the mud, a soft, wet pillow.

"Come." I extend my hands toward her, holding them in place until she has the strength to reach over and take them. I drag her out of the water, up the riverbank, and hide her behind the tall grass. She is fully clothed, wet and breathless. Her dress clings to her tiny frame and she shivers so loudly I think the boats might hear and come back for her. I can feel the warmth as the crops burn, the sound of desperate people pleading drowned out by the sound of destruction.

"*Quoi?* What?" It's all I can seem to whisper, but she sets her head down on her muddy hands and I see a bruise the size of a man's hand forming along her jaw, invading her eye. But she says nothing. We wait in silence as two more boats pass, these ones quiet, resigned to whatever awaits them when the sun wakes. I take her hand, forcing her to her feet. We stumble together through the grass, both of us looking behind.

The fire is dead and the children sit behind my wife, guarded by her outstretched arms, her wide eyes frightened. The hide door to the hut sits open behind them. When Hélène sees them, she stops, unsure, looking back to me, hesitating.

"*Ma famille,*" I explain, and her face twists into an unnatural grimace.

"They, they, they . . ." She stops, not moving, not speaking, just looking at my children, who have begun to peek out from behind their mother.

"They killed Father." She drops to the ground, her tiny body convulsing in sobs.

I don't know what to do. I've never seen such a display.

My wife, resigned to watching until now, tells me to sit with the children as she gathers Hélène's head and places it onto her lap. She has never met Gilbert or Hélène, having left the trading to me.

"They make me nervous, these pale people," she had said the one and only time I asked if she would like to go with me to Gilbert's. But now, after the moon slips under the horizon and the first light of day paints the clouds red and purple, she sits with the yellow-haired daughter of my good friend in her lap, humming until the weakened girl falls asleep, her wet dress no match for the tiredness that comes with shock and grief.

My children sit and whisper, rubbing their smoke-sore eyes, pointing to the girl. The little one still has berry juice on her fingers and, I notice in the light of morning, around her lips. The blackberries lie strewn on the other side of the fire. I must have knocked them over in the night. She moves over and grabs a few, stuffing them into her mouth and handing one each to her brothers and sisters. Despite their protests, I herd them into the birchbark tent, but my wife refuses to leave the sleeping Hélène, so I take a seat behind her, my legs outstretched, my back holding the weight of these women as they sleep.

"She shivers," my wife whispers. "Go inside and get a fur.

Throw it to me, but stay inside. I need to take these clothes off her and wrap her to keep sickness away. And send out our oldest girl."

Hélène has been sleeping long enough for the sun to be sitting above where the tall grasses used to be. The only things remaining are the charred stumps of corn and grain turned to ash in the wind. I return to the hut and throw a fur out to her as instructed. When I am told I can come out, Hélène is awake and sitting up, her shoulders slumped, wrapped in the hides, my oldest daughter sitting rubbing her back and cooing, just like her mother. Hélène's pale-yellow dress is hung over the racks used to dry fish. The fish lie on the ground in a perfect line. My wife has started a fire, moving Hélène's feet closer to get warm. Hélène looks up when I approach and starts to cry. My daughter holds her closer, taking one of her pale hands in hers. I see them now, the two of them, and realize that they are around the same age.

"They set everything on fire, it smelled so bad. Father refused to leave and refused to say an oath to their king. They shot him." She hangs her head and the crying starts again. "We were happy here," she sobs.

My daughter, not understanding the words but understanding the girl, cradles her head in her arms, rocking her and singing a soft song.

"He was the first and the last to refuse. They dragged him to the village, laid him out on the ground." She raises her head to look at me. Her eyes, normally so blue and happy, are red, her cheeks blotched. "Let this be a lesson, they said, and they left him there to burn and put us on boats."

I translate the best I can and watch the face of my wife sadden.

"He was my father, my only family."

The little ones come out from the tent, and the smallest girl, her fingers still stained, gathers the rest of the strewn berries from the ground and offers them to Hélène, her fat little hand full. Hélène nods and takes them. She takes a berry and slowly chews. The dark-blue juice leaks down the crease that runs from her mouth to her chin, which seems to have grown overnight, making her look older. My beautiful berry-stained child takes a seat on her lap and plays with the hair that has escaped the yellow braid worked by my wife. Hélène smiles for the first time.

"What have they done with the people?" I ask in my best French.

"Sent to find new homes. This is what they told us. New

homes where traitors would be welcomed." She rests her chin on the top of my daughter's head.

"And you?" I ask. "What do you intend?"

My wife has started to cook and the children, having so easily adjusted to the presence of a stranger at our camp, play and make noise. I shush them so I can hear any voices that may be near, carried on the wind and water. But there are none.

"I don't know. I felt like I was betraying my father by staying on that boat," she says with a sigh. "And I have nothing. No one and nothing."

I translate for my wife.

"Then she will come with us to the winter camp. It will be hard work for her, but she will get used to it." My wife says this as if there will be no protest from the others. She sees my apprehension. "Don't look so worried. She will get used to it and they will understand. Our people know what it feels like to be removed from the only home they've known. They will find sympathy in their hearts." My wife pours water, heated over the fire, into a wooden bowl, placing fish in it to soften before passing it to Hélène. "She can decide what she would like to do once the snow has melted back into the rivers. Perhaps her people will return." She shrugs.

I'm not as confident as my wife, but she predicted two boys

and five girls would come from her womb and she was right each time.

"You tell her now. Tell her what we offer. And tell her that she will have to learn our tongue now. I won't learn hers." My wife stands and walks to where the fish are drying, holding them to her nose before laying them on a hide and wrapping them.

I watch Hélène as she stares into the flames of our small fire, sipping the tea with blackberries floating on top.

"Hélène?" Her name is not as lovely from my tongue as it was from her father's, but she looks up, waiting for me. "You can come with us if you wish, stay with us for the winter. Then you can decide what will become of you."

She tilts her head to the side and for a moment I think I have said the wrong French words. But then she nods.

"Merci. Merci."

HOMECOMING

S he looks at me, her head tilted to the side, her eyes searching for the familiar eyes of her father. Her wrinkles are
new, and she has grey in her hair. It wasn't there the last time
I saw her, but my nose is still her nose. She takes my face in
her hands and nestles my chin where her hands meet above
the wrist, holding me softly, turning my head from side to side,
whispering in her language of soft consonants.

A lot has changed in eleven years. I am taller and wider
than I was then. I have stubble growing on my chin. Not a
lot, but enough to add to the strangeness of the meeting. The
last time she saw me, I was small, waving from the back of an
aluminum motorboat that droned loudly and rattled my teeth
when it bounced over the waves. I remember laughing and

waving. From the water, I watched as my mother ran along the thin slip of sand between the ocean and the forest, waving her arms in the air. Her face was strained, but I couldn't hear her shouts over the sound of the motor. She became smaller as we approached open water. I thought we would turn back, and I would get to tell her about jumping over waves and the taste of salt water on my lips. But we didn't turn back. I watched, my eyes narrowed, searching, as the figure of my mother faded into the trees behind her. I've been practising my story every day since—the story of the waves and the way the water turned my summer skin white with salt. I used to practise in her words, but now I can't find them. I've waited so long to tell her. I've never seen a return. I've heard stories, of course, hushed voices in the middle of the night, the story weaving its way down the line of beds, the blankets scratchy and threadbare by your eleventh year. You only get one. But they were just stories. Some, emboldened by these tales, ran away, trying to get home. Most of the time they ended up back beneath their scratchy blanket, the tips of their fingers and toes dark from the cold in the winter or their tiny brown bodies littered with bug bites in summer. A few didn't come back at all. Charles, a simple boy prone to tall tales but big like a giant, told us that the nuns made him dig a hole in the back once, just beyond the fence that kept us in, behind the garden that grew food we weren't permitted to eat. He said it was just big enough to hold Hagar, a girl who had gone missing just two days before. But it was too terrifying to think about. Hagar, under the ground, cold and alone. Her sister refused to believe it, and when she went home the year before I did, she was confident her sister would greet her.

My mother gently pats both my cheeks then leaves me on my own, sitting in an old wooden chair outside the door of the tiny shack. It's new, this shack with its tarpaper walls and shingled roof. It doesn't look new, but it wasn't here the last time I was, so therefore it's new. When I was still their son, we lived under the tree limbs and birchbark, animal hides covering the bare ground. We watched the stars travel across the sky in the summer and listened to tall tales of giant men with hair like the bear in the winter. We collected berries and stained our lips red with their juices. We hunted rabbits for stew and cooked fish over a fire. Before the boat took me away, I was about to go on my first hunt.

"These deer are not like your small rabbits. These animals are big, and they are smart. You need to be smarter." My father slid the feather into the small groove at the end of the perfectly fashioned stick. "You need to be smarter and quieter and smaller. You understand?"

I nodded, watching him connect the chiselled stone to the other end of the stick with rope made of dried seagrass. But I never got to go on my first real hunt, and aside from a few foxes at the school, I've never seen a large animal. Monsters yes—animals no.

"Savages live like that." This is what they told us at the school. "We have been called upon by God to civilize you." It was said so much, it became meaningless to me, and I still don't understand if they succeeded. Am I civilized? They told me I was, but their words were often marked with falsehood.

I'm not sure if I'm supposed to follow my mother inside her small home, so I stay, the clothes I went into the school with tucked in a bag at my feet along with a Bible, no bigger than the palm of my hand. It's how they taught us to read, this tiny book of stories of a vengeful God and benevolent Messiah. They are nothing like our stories, the ones I only half remember. The clothes I have on now, the same ones I wore each day working in the fields, pulling potatoes and swatting at flies, are dirty and they smell. It was a long walk around the water instead of across it. But I'm here now.

I don't know how long I sit there, listening as she works away inside. When I left on the boat all those years ago, I had three older brothers and a father. But now I see no one, hear only her work and the wind. The sun is about to duck behind a stand of tall pine trees when he emerges, his figure still tall but slightly stooped. He has a few rabbits flung over his shoulder and a rifle tucked under his arm. He stops at the tree line to look at me. His walk is slower and more crooked than I remember, his legs slightly bowed.

"Father?"

"Nujj," he whispers softly as I stand to greet him.

"Nujj," I repeat back. The word has become clumsy on my tongue from years of disuse.

He smiles and lays the rabbit at my feet beside the bag and takes my face in his hands, moving my head from side to side, inspecting me, the same way she did. He lets go, steps back, smiles and nods, before bending down to pick up the rabbits and heading inside. He speaks to me, but I don't know what he says. I start to cry as he ducks through the door, waving me in, beckoning me to follow. There, under a low ceiling, the table is set for three.

THE VIRGIN AND THE BEAR

I had a dream once that a Bear battled the Virgin Mary for my soul. It was just after my grandfather died and the Virgin stood there, at the foot of my bed, shrouded in blue and white, hands outstretched, her pale face, a fallacy of history and mythology. Outside, the Bear beat against the door in desperation, roared and then went quiet.

A clap of thunder ripped me from my dream, the sound of blood rushing through my veins pounded in my ears. The rain, like the bony fingers of a fairy-tale witch, tapped incessantly on the bedroom window. But I was fine—a little sweaty from fear, a little weaker from holding myself stiff, but fine. And in the quiet after the storm, unable to shake the fear entirely, I stayed awake, waiting until the grey sky cast light through the slats of the blinds and shadows bent and slipped under the door.

I waited for the Bear or the Virgin to take claim. But neither did, or so I thought.

As the years passed, the dream faded, the Virgin became nothing more than a hazy shadow of what she was, the Bear a quiet roar in the back of my memory. And as I grew older, I wandered to places where there were bears and went without seeing one. I roamed the woods where my grandfather and I used to roam, I walked the trails of my new home, on the other side of the continent where the sun shone and the black bears lived, wandering among trees so high that they touched the clouds. I wandered to countries and cities where the Virgin was revered, and she was everywhere. I saw her in cathedrals, on pedestals, her hair in Venice. So I yielded to the Virgin although I never felt the divine presence testified to by so many. Yet, as a woman of twenty-eight, I was so convinced that the Virgin had won that, when I was in Rome, I bought my dead grandmother a rosary, painted glass, white with tiny blue bellflowers. My grandmother's rosary was red with wooden beads. She had been buried with it, entwined in her fingers like crooked tree roots taking possession. When I tired of my travels, I laid the new rosary on my grandmother's grave, where it was promptly stolen.

"YOU BRING THE BAD weather with you. I never saw anything like it." My grandfather smiled at me as he stood with his hands on his hips and watched as the fog rolled in off the bay. It leapt over the tops of the pines and sank to the surface of the lake before rising again, an acrobatic dance over lakes and hills. "The fog follows you, girl." He clicked his tongue and walked toward a parting in the grass. "Looks like the right kind of sky for a storm. Let's pray it doesn't thunder." He laughed under his breath.

I looked to the sky, the tip of the canoe still in my hand, and felt the electric fear that always accompanied the thought of thunder. I pulled the canoe ashore, tucking it under some brush before running to catch up. The lake crossing was quiet in the morning before the afternoon winds lifted the water into little waves, small but strong, enough to make the paddle hard on the arms and back, especially for a skinny eleven-year-old. *Made of toothpicks and sawdust, you are. A good wind would blow you away to the four corners of the earth*, my grandmother used to say.

When we left, before the sun was up, there had been no sign of fog. Here it was, thick as heavy cream, floating past us on its way from one bay to another; this little slip of land in between and the narrow lake that sat in the middle couldn't stop its journey to the open water. In the summer, this little piece of land, separating the two bays, drew thunderstorms like flies to rotting fruit. I hated those storms. The electricity scorched the sky and bounced off the lake with a snap. I cowered under the arm of my grandfather as he sat on the small step of his now-disintegrated cabin, marvelling at the power of Mother Nature—encouraging me to marvel with him.

"I guess we'll follow the fog," he said as he used his walking stick to part the tall grass at the edge of the lake.

"Won't we get lost?"

"Only if we didn't know where we were going. I know this place as well as I know the tiny freckles on your grandmother's nose." He bent down and touched the end of my nose. "Just like these ones." I reached up to scratch where the wool from his mitten had left an itch behind.

He could wander these woods on the darkest night, without even the moon. Later in life, when my father was receding into memory, unable to remember the present, he told me stories about how, as a boy, he had travelled these same trails when he was my age, leading white men from America through the woods in search of deer to kill. In the back closet of the room that had formerly belonged to my father and his brothers, behind a broken piece of plywood acting as a wall, I once found an old poster with a cartoon Indian on it. *Hunting with a Real Red Indian. Book Your Trip Now*, it read, in big, impressive letters along the top. I asked my grandmother about it, but she sighed and told me to put it back where I found it and that we didn't do that anymore. I put it back, but when I went to show my dad a few weeks later, the poster was gone.

I stayed close and watched the backs of my grandfather's feet. The muddy bottoms of his shoes and the imprint they left in the ground guided me through the fog. The grass moved with the breeze, bending and swaying. This time of year, the grass made a crunching sound if there was a particularly strong gust of wind. And each time, he turned to tell me that the crunch was the sound of a bear trying to sneak up on us. I knew, somewhere in my child mind, that he was joking, but still, I strained my neck, looking over the grass, half expecting the brown face of a bear staring back at me.

The trail was narrow, a footpath really, twisting and weaving its way through the grass until it met the tree line at the top of the hill. The fog moved on in front of us in its race to the water, making it easier to see where we were going. We walked quietly, the silence interrupted only by our breathing and the sound of our feet touching the earth. When my grandfather stopped to take a deep breath, *breathing in the wind*, he'd say, I stopped to do the same. Long before you can see the bay, you can smell it. The cool, salty air in the lungs and heavy on the tongue. The wet you can almost feel on the inside of your nose.

"That, my dear girl, is a smell that's sewn into your soul, stitched in your blood. People in the middle of this land don't have it. And if someday you find yourself somewhere without salt water, you'll smell it still, that's how rooted it is in us, the smell of this water." He told me this each time we walked this trail, but I never tired of hearing it. Now, older and as educated as I am, I still think there is something magical about a soul made of salt water.

"Pay attention," he chided when a branch he was holding snapped back and caught my cheek. "No daydreaming in the woods, girl. You'll get yourself hurt or lost."

I nodded and rubbed the side of my cheek. It stung, but the irritation was brief because there in front of me, down a little sandy hill, was the bay. The greyness of the sky was reflected in the water, the wind chopping it into tiny bits of white, foam-topped waves. The gulls squawked. They looked like kites on a string in the wind before they settled on the water or a nearby boulder. My eyes followed along the shore as it bent out toward open water, the sandy brown cliffs growing higher but looking smaller the farther out you looked. I loved exploring the caves dug out of the cliffs by the force of tidal water. But there was no time today for exploring; the tide had turned and was coming toward us. Soon the caves would disappear under the water.

"Next time, we'll come out for a day or two and explore the caves, I promise," he said.

While the tide was still far enough away, exposing the stones and mud, there was work to do. I wasn't sure what; he hadn't told me. Sometimes when we came, we collected seaweed to fertilize the garden or searched out the really good stuff so we could dry it on the wood stove and then eat it, salty and crisp. But today we walked past the line where the bay deposited the driftwood and fishing debris, past the seaweed and the first line of small stones. Past the larger stones, our feet sinking into them, making it hard to walk.

"Come on, then, leave those rocks alone."

I liked to collect the rocks, take them home and put them in old jars or make trails in the front garden. Trails of rocks, blue, orange and white. I still secretly liked to think that the white ones were shark teeth, even though I was old enough now to know better. The fog had wandered out to sit on top of the water, slowly whirling its way to the Atlantic as I ran to catch up. Grandfather bent and lifted something from a small puddle of water that had gathered in a shallow pool, the bay leaving a small part of itself behind. He wiped it on his pants and held it up to the dull light of the hidden sun. The rock was out of place here among the grey-blues and brown, and it wasn't like the others scattered on the beach. It was a striking blue. Looking into the shallow pool, I saw more, many more. Different shapes and sizes, but all the same wonderful blue.

"Go ahead and grab one. The sea should have softened their sharp edges by now."

I reached into the cold water, a small blue rock between pink fingers, the chill moving up my neck and settling in under my hairline.

"How are the rocks so blue?" I whispered, turning one over in my hand.

"They're not rocks, silly girl. It's sea glass."

I dropped mine back into the shallow pond. The blue rock skipped off a stone and was absorbed into the rest of them.

"Sea glass?" I looked down and saw the last of the ripples reach the edge of the tide pool.

"I take those bottles your grandmother saves and break them on the rocks and let the sea shape them." He laughed even harder at the baffled look on my face. "Look, this one is shaped like a bear, your grandmother's clan."

He started to hand it to me, but I moved my hand away.

"It won't cut you anymore, the sea has made sure of that. Take it, it's yours."

He stood there, the small blue object lying in his palm.

"Would I give you something that would hurt you?" he said, moving his outstretched hand even closer until I gingerly picked up the blue piece of glass.

He reached into the pool for another as I tested the edges for sharpness. It *was* shaped like a bear, the edges of the glass softened to the point where it looked as if the little creature might just stand up and walk off the edge of my palm.

"How did you make it look like a bear?" I asked.

"Oh, I didn't do that. I break the glass and the sea does the rest. She decides what will become of it. I just leave the pieces here for her." He bent to the little pool and began to collect the glass, inspecting each piece before placing it in a leather bag tied to his belt.

"Why?"

"Why what?"

"Why do you break glass and put it in the bay?"

"I sell them. It's a small profit, but it keeps your grandmother and me in tea and sugar."

"Sell them? To who?"

The bear was warming in my hand as we left the little shallow pool, now empty of blue, and moved along the shore. A few minutes later, he stopped and crouched down again. This time, the glass was green.

"Tourists, artists. They think there is something magical in broken glass. They put it back together to make something new. Or maybe they find bears." He laughed to himself and pointed to my closed fist, the blue bear safely inside.

"It seems silly to break a bottle that you can use, just to make broken glass." I opened my clenched hand, the bear still there, still blue.

"There can be beauty in destruction. Something formed

one way, made new again. There needs to be more of that in the world." He put his palm under my chin, lifting it up so that I was looking into his dark-brown eyes. "Don't you agree?"

I shrugged and he let go, reaching for the blue bear, but I was too quick and closed my fingers around it.

"See, even you love the beauty of it, this broken thing." He smiled and started whistling the same tune he always whistled, and moved on to the next tide pool.

That day, before the tide crawled back to the shoreline, we filled his small leather sack with sea glass, blue, green, white and a few rare pieces of red from my grandmother's favourite perfume bottle.

"We'll bring some more bottles down with us the next time we walk. Don't lose the bear—your grandmother will want to see that one. And I will tell you a secret. That rosary she prays with"—he leaned in as if telling a secret even the gulls shouldn't know—"one of them has a bear etched into it. A tiny little bear. She put it there with a sewing needle. Don't tell her I told you." He put his old finger up to his lips, smiled, turned and walked down the shore. I ran to catch up as the roll of thunder, miles off, warned us of its imminent arrival.

I never told my grandmother that I knew her secret, but I

did sneak a peek once when she was napping in her chair, her knitted afghan wrapped around her legs, her head resting on the side of the rocker. She slept a lot before the cancer took her. Her rosary sat on the little stand by the window beside the small statue of the Virgin a local priest had given her, long before I was part of her world.

I took each bead into my hand, under the watchful eyes of the Virgin, looking for the bear. Halfway through, I found it etched into a single bead, so small and delicate. The red of the wood had rubbed soft, but held up to the light, it had a hint of shine. I placed it back on the little stand, trying to remember exactly how it had sat, arranging them, then rearranging them, when she let out a little snort and opened her eyes.

"Tea, Nan?"

"Yes, please."

She stretched, yawned and reached for her rosary, just where she'd left it.

THE DAY IS STILL, the humidity creeping into every crevice—the backs of my knees, between my breasts, the back of my neck where aging skin has started to gather. The air has pasted the tiny golden cross to my chest, a gift to each grand-child when they turned sixteen. The blue bear, once forgotten, is now remembered after an afternoon of cleaning out my mother's attic. Sometime in my teenage years I placed it in my memory box, an old cookie tin where all my treasures ended up. Now it sits tucked into the pocket of my purse.

An eeriness settles over me as I drive to the old brick school. I can't help but wonder at people's desire to visit places like this, places that hold so much grief and horror. But I've been to Europe, bought tickets to see Auschwitz. I visited Asia and toured the killing fields of Cambodia. I never really under-stood what drew me to these places. But this is different, this is a history that flows through my blood. My grandmother lived here, brought here when she was seven, permitted to leave when she was twelve. I have a reason to be here.

I park my car and buy my ticket at the bottom of the hill and walk the rest of the way, meeting the tour guide at the main doors. The doors are imposing, the cross carved into one, a stack of books carved into the other. I don't pay much attention to the lecture at the beginning. My eyes are busy roaming the crevices in the red brick, observing the peeling paint from the original windows, and the weather-beaten grey wood exposed in most places. At the corners, the foundation has started to crumble. The rock, exhausted from holding so much weight for so long, rests in the tall grass that grows around the edges.

As we explore, the voice of the tour guide echoes off the empty rooms. Dust enters through open windows and settles on the pine floors. No beds line up in the rooms the way you see in the pictures, no tin bowls or desks with pencils in the little notch at the top that you read about in books. Only the chapel still holds the past, and the cupboard under the stairs.

"We're not supposed to talk about it," says the guide, a boy no older than twenty if I were to make a bet. "But they held the bad ones in that cupboard, the misbehavers, deviants." He says the last word proudly, as if it's the first time he's used it out loud after practising for weeks. "They would be put there until they confessed." There is something unsettling about how easy it is to move on to the next thing, to consider something so upsetting so quickly. But the tour is only forty-five minutes and we have to keep moving. Others are waiting.

"And you will see here, in the chapel, the pews where the children prayed each morning before breakfast and each evening before bed." The tour guide turns, making the sign of the cross and bending at his knee before allowing us to wander on our own for a bit, so long as we stay in the public areas, leaving alone the rooms with rope strung across their entry-ways. I shake at the thought of the rooms behind the rope.

I sit down on one of the pews, the hard wood uncomfort-able, and wonder if my grandmother ever sat here. I wonder if she looked up at the same picture of the Virgin that still stands above the aging altar. The picture is a familiar one, the Virgin, her head tilted to the side, one hand outstretched, bestowing mercy on a child. The paint is faded, her blue cloak greyer now. Her smile is thin, but it is her, the same Virgin that visited me when I was barely out of childhood.

I have a habit of looking for heretical art in churches. I've always loved the way people bestow their own stories on those who are trying to destroy them. How, as hard as they try, the conquerors can never really erase the vanquished. They always leave a trace, no matter how small. In my trav-els in Europe, I was always excited to find these small signs, to commiserate with the stonemasons, the Celts, the Druids, those who refused to be written out of history. But here, in this chapel where my grandmother was forced to her knees to pray, I want more than anything to find something rebellious. But there is nothing, no petroglyphs etched in the wood, no pencil scratchings on the walls. Nothing to show you who they were before they were brought here in an effort to change them into something entirely new.

"Are you okay?" An older woman, her handkerchief extended, sits down beside me. She rubs her hand up and down my back, her free hand in mine. "I remember when this school was open." Her hand stops mid-back, resting there. "If we'd only known. You keep that hanky, dear." She stands and makes her way down the pew and out of the chapel, the wood under her feet creaking. The absence of her hand on my back gives me a chill, running up my spine and encircling my head. I stuff the damp cloth in the pocket of my jacket and lean forward, ready to leave. I place my hands on the seat, my fingers curving under, touching the underside of the pew.

"Ouch." I lift my hand, a wood splinter sunk deep in the tip of my finger, the red of blood dotting the place where it entered. I grab the end and pull it from my flesh before sticking the end of my finger in my mouth, the taste of iron coating my tongue. The bleeding stopped, I reach back down, carefully this time, to find the offending wood. My finger, tender and sore, follows the rough engraving in the wood. It is something, but what I can't tell.

"We're about to move on to the grounds. We'll explore the gardens and then the barn, which is now a museum and bookstore. Just a few minutes more in here," the tour guide announces.

The metallic taste of blood still in my mouth, I slip to the floor, lying down in the narrowness. I use the light of my phone to see that under the pew, etched out of the wood by a stone perhaps, is the figure of a star, and beside it a rough tree, the pine limbs extending out to almost touch the head of an owl. At least, I think it is an owl. The figures lined up along the underside of the pew are roughly etched into the wood, all small and old. Some are rubbed smooth. Some I recognize from books and stone drawings, some cartoonish and others undecipherable. I push my feet against the floor to move up to see the others, and there, near the end of the pew, is a bear.

THE RAIN THAT FELL earlier this morning has settled into the earth as I stand at the start of the trail. The last of the storm clouds blow by, taking the fog and the sound of thunder with them. It doesn't bother me anymore, this thunder. It's taken decades, but I've become used to it now. I reach in to grasp my grandfather's bear, buried deep in my pocket.

The trail is wider than it was in the past. A provincial trail, maintained with loose gravel that has become hard-packed and damp, like the air. To get here, there is no need of a canoe, no need to drive around a bay and then cross a lake. Now, an asphalt double lane, marked with potholes and crumbling at the edges, runs between the lake and the bay, taking tourists to the villages that used to be accessible only by boat. The old fishing shacks are art galleries now, the old church, abandoned by the faithless, a café serving cappuccino and red velvet cup-cakes. I wonder what my grandfather would have thought about all this, his trail now walked on by so many, his sea glass beach used by teens to drink beer and families to picnic and set off fireworks. His cabin, crumpled, the remnants covered in grass and brambles. Even I can't find it anymore. Either my memory has failed me or Mother Nature is taking back what is rightfully hers.

Standing here in the damp, I think I can see him in front of me, his carved walking stick dimpling the earth. Just far enough ahead that I'll never catch up. Someone has placed a sign, nailed to a crooked post, warning BEWARE OF BEARS. Somewhere in the back of my mind I can hear my grand-father's voice warning me that bears would find me a tasty treat, as his heavy laugh works its way out of my mouth. I shiver before reaching around and taking the gold-plated cross from around my neck, unclasping it for the last time. The bear sign is low and leaning, and I can easily drape the necklace over it. I don't look back, there's no need, a lifetime of searching has taught me that nothing is behind you that you won't find up ahead.

I'm the only one here today, as far as I can tell. There are no other cars in the gravel parking lot. It's November—warm, but still November. The people enter a weird hibernation this time of year. They disappear behind warm fires and closed curtains for months at a time, drinking tea and making bread, playing cards and making babies. Then one day in the spring, a day not defined by any calendar, they emerge, refreshed and ready for the light and warmth. They won't go out in November. That's just not how it's done. Thirty years in the California sun has made me forget.

My boots crunch the gravel and echo, a cathedral of trees sending my own sounds back to me. And there is the smell, the heavy scent of salt. I stop and lift my nose as high as I can, breathing it in. I may have forgotten how to hibernate, but the salt water is still in my blood. Halfway down the trail, the woods thin out. Dead trees lean and decay. A tiny frog jumps across the path in front of me and I stop to let him pass. I try to follow him, but his camouflaged body disappears under some ferns. I was so enchanted with the journey of a small tree frog that I haven't heard her approach. But there is no mistaking it now, as a loud thump followed closely by another makes me turn.

She stands there, her body blocking the trail. She's quiet, with the exception of her breath, which hangs in a thick mist on the air. She looks at me and bows her head before shaking off the rain. Her fur glistens blue-black in the few bands of sun that manage to cut through the trees. The wild smell of her reaches my nose, this is how close she is. She lifts her head, sniffing, before picking up one giant paw and placing it down with a force that I can feel in my feet and again as it reaches my heart and again as my teeth chatter. I can stand still or run toward the water. I decide to stand.

"Good morning, Muin," I whisper.

She picks her head up and looks directly at me, a growl

escaping from the depths of her throat. I can feel my sweat soaking through and spreading. The cool drops of rain falling off needles and leaves give no comfort. My hands are balled so tightly into fists, I can't feel the individual fingers anymore. Inside, my heart is beating so fast, for a moment I think it might stop altogether. I clear my throat.

"We're family, you and I."

She stares at me.

I move to pull the blue bear out from under my nylon rain jacket. The movement makes her sway her giant body back and forth, her eyes trained on me. I hold out the blue piece of sea-weathered glass. I don't know if she looks at it, my fear seems to have taken the memory and discarded it, but she moves awkwardly onto her back legs, opens her mouth, her teeth exposed, and roars. I swear the trees shake with the force of it. Then, with a grunt, she turns and heads back into the forest.

I can't move, the blue bear stuck to the sweat of my palm, my heart beating in my neck, my fingers, and I can feel every internal organ switching back on. I start to breathe again as she stops and takes one last look at me before disappearing into the thicket. I wait there, perfectly still, until I can't see or hear her any longer.

I reach the shore. I don't know how, exactly. I assume I must have walked, but I may have run. I remember standing, the waves licking the toes of my boots before my heart returns to its natural rhythm. I slowly uncurl my fingers, the blood returning to the tips, making them pink again. Rain has started to fall, and off in the distance the clouds roar with the returning thunder. I lick the salt off my lips as I watch the waves crash on the boulders. There is a peace just then. The water still washes ashore, but I can't hear it; the gulls are quiet and the thunder roars meekly off beyond the horizon.

ASHES

Everything is gone, black patches of ash where our homes stood just yesterday, the earth still smouldering, sputtering in the rain. The acrid smell hangs off each raindrop, scattering the scent of ruin as it hits the ground. I am old now, too old, and far too tired of the games these men play. They wander, the ash sticking to the bottoms of their boots, stopping to take photos, posing in front of dead fires, smiles on their faces.

They stole my words, brought back three sons and one daughter wounded and scarred. And now they steal the last thing they can, the very land where I want to rest my old body, where I was to be buried with the ones who went before. How will they find me now when my time comes? Even my death has been stolen. The tears fall as naturally as the rain, quiet and full. These men are cruel to bring an old woman, to show me everything I've ever known scattered to the wind or sunk in the mud. They will make me tell the story of our loss.

"It's for your own good, old woman."

The man smiles at me, and I don't even think he knows he is being cruel. I watch a thin trail of smoke blend into the approaching fog before I sit down hard on the ground, with no family to take my arm and help me make the transition from standing to sitting. I take the warm ash in my hands, smelling it, breathing it in. It smells of sixty-two winters, of sixteen children born and nine who lived. The ashes used to smell of mornings, of new beginnings, another day to walk with the earth, to sit with my grandchildren and listen to their laughter. Now, these ashes only smell of grief. I look over at the scorched patch of earth where my daughter slept, cooked and loved. She will mourn when I tell her. The men stand quietly, watching me, thinking I will understand.

"Come, old woman. It's time to head back to the Mainland, to your new home." The man reaches under my arm and yanks me up until I am standing, a bruise forming where my arm meets my old body.

"How could you have done this?" I would like to sound angry, but instead my voice cracks, betraying me.

"You Indians, why do you prefer to live like animals? We are doing you a favour. You're poor, these cabins aren't homes, they're not fit for man nor beast. There are schools on the Mainland, indoor toilets. It's the 1960s, you don't need to live like this anymore."

How foolish he is, the yellow hair curled under his cap, his whiskers struggling to poke through his childlike skin.

The man pulls me to the boat and places me at the back, alone, while they take a few more pictures to prove their good deed. The water sloshes against the side of the boat as I take my seat on the hard bench, the airy foam a beautiful white. I reach in, letting my knotted fingers ripple the water, gathering the foam in my palm as we push away from the land. I lift my hand to my face, the water dripping and staining my dress as I breathe in deep and blow the foam back into the air. I will miss this water that holds our stories.

I know then that I can't be the one to tell them that it's gone. It can't be me. I stand up at the end of the small vessel. With the slowness that comes with age, I turn to face the water, using my hands to steady my old body. I will not face them, not now. The men yell for me to sit, but their voices are drowned out by the call of the water. As we reach the centre of the channel, I feel one of the men tug on the bottom of my dress, and faintly, like listening through a seashell, I hear them tell me once again to sit. But I know it's my time. The wind caresses my face and I let myself fall. There is no pain as the water welcomes me.

The voices whisper, *Come and find peace with us.*

WOLVES

In the quiet moments when my body is so tired that even my teeth stop chattering, I'm almost able to convince myself that I don't have a dirty face or chipped fingernails. My black hair—cut short with a jackknife at a truck stop somewhere in New Brunswick—is long and shiny again. The cheeks that belonged to my grandmother and were passed down to me sit high and proud. I can remember in the quiet moments, but they're so few out here where the cars move incessantly, where the buses brake and the partiers stumble down the snow-covered sidewalks throwing drunken slurs in a language I barely understand. A few nights after I got here, one of them tipped the cup of Tim Hortons tea right out of my hand. I watched as it melted the dirty snow. It had taken me all day to gather enough change to buy it and they laughed as they stumbled past me.

The people at the shelter can't understand. They're too busy trying to save me to ask why I'm here. They see my dirty brown face and assume they know all about me. I liked the house with the blue door and the people inside it, but I have to find her, that's why I left, that's why I'm here. The night I snuck away was cool, not cold yet, the lingering warmth of early fall still on the breeze. The branches of the maples creaked in the gentle wind as the last of the leaves came to rest on the perfectly manicured lawns and the paved sidewalks, sidewalks that led to driveways with Volvos and basketball nets. Now, the wind is angry and cold. It whips at my face, my cheeks red and burning. The cold itself seeps in through the layers of dirty clothes, soaking into my bones.

The blue door had a knocker, the kind you see in old movies. It was a howling wolf, his neck outstretched, baying to an invisible moon. A piece of iron, moulded to look like a tree branch, hung from his neck. I reached up to touch the wrought iron, to feel the grooves of the wolf's mane. It reminded me of the stories my grandmother told about wolves, how they move in packs, depending on one another, protecting each other. I didn't get a chance to knock before the door opened, the interior light fading into the muted dusk of late September.

"It was here when we bought the place," he told me, his hand still on the inside knob, his face turned toward my arm, still outstretched, reaching for the wolf. I let my arm fall to my side.

"Darren." He reached out to shake my hand.

"Melissa." I took his hand. It was warm and his shake friendly. A garbage bag with all my possessions sat at my feet, my backpack still slung over one shoulder.

"And you know my wife, Catherine." She smiled and wiped her hands with a dishtowel.

"Hello again, Melissa. I know it's hard, and I wish we were meeting again under better circumstances, but I am happy to see you."

"Come in, Melissa. No need to stand outside in the chill when we can be comfortable inside." Darren stepped aside to give me room.

I paused for just a second to admire the knocker once more as Catherine and the social worker reviewed the plans my grandmother had made months before. Four weeks later, when I left that house—my grief still heavy in my heart, and burdened by naive hope—the knocker made the quietest sound as the door closed, the iron tree branch gently thumping against the stop. I waited to see if anyone heard it, but no one came.

The smell of beef stew, hot and thick, came at me from down the hall as I dropped my garbage bag on the floor. While they talked details, I glanced into the rooms I could see. In the living room, a couch, blue and unstained, sat in front of the largest television I'd ever seen. I couldn't see into the kitchen at the end of the hall, but the smell of food let me know it was there. My head was still hazy from the events of the last couple of days and their words fell into my ears but went unheard. I had too much and not enough to think about, all at the same time. I didn't even hear my own name until Catherine placed her hand on my shoulder and turned me toward her.

"Melissa?" She smiled sympathetically. "It's going to be okay. We're happy to have you here with us.

"I miss her too. Your grandmother was a very special lady. Did she ever tell you that she saved my life? I hope that, in some small way, I can help you too. It is the least I can do for her." She bent, took my garbage bag of clothes and headed up the stairs. "I'll show you to your room. I hope you like it."

I slung my backpack over my shoulder and followed her. "Thank you," I whispered when she showed me to a room at the top of the stairs. It was small: a bed, dresser, desk, everything in various shades of purple. Off to the side of the desk was a door leading to my own bathroom, a narrow shower and toilet.

"If you'd like to have a shower, I've got some soap and stuff for you. And there are towels on the little shelf."

"Thank you," I said again, the only words I could find in the muddled mess of my thoughts. The water was hot, hotter than it needed to be, but it felt good. When I looked in the full-length mirror, my skin was red, and my long hair was plastered against my face and skull. I couldn't find a comb, so I used my fingers to untangle my hair.

"Well," I whispered to myself as I sat on the edge of the bed and pulled on my tights and loose sweater, a Salvation Army special. I put on my socks, the ones my grandmother made me, dark-grey wool with white stripes along the top. And then I waited. I wasn't sure if I had to wait for them to come get me or if I was supposed to go downstairs. My stomach growled at the smell of stew when I peeked my head out the door. There was no one in the hallway, so I decided to wait. I reached for my backpack at the end of the bed. I dug down to the bottom until my fingers grazed the envelope. It was old, the edges were bent, and the lines where it was folded were brown. Everything at my grandmother's house was eventually tarnished by cigarette smoke and my letter was no different. I held it up to my nose and breathed in the noxious smell of nicotine and tar, which filled me with so many memories.

Dear Melissa . . . She wrote in half cursive and half printed letters, the words angled in the way people write when they are left-handed. The letters were tidy, as if she took her time, considering each word carefully before committing it to paper. She was healthy and working, she wrote. Soon she would send for me. That had been three years ago, and it was the last letter she had sent, postmarked Montreal.

The house was quiet, the occasional light from a passing car sliding across the wall. When they didn't come for me and the colour purple became too much, I quietly made my way down the stairs. I found them in the dining room, the smell of my mint shampoo mixing with beef and the unmistakable smell of biscuits. The table was set and they were talking quietly. The little one sat silent, waiting. His brown eyes watched me. His hair was cut short, too short, like the kids who got lice in school each year. They'd waited for me before eating.

"I'm sorry," I stammered, embarrassed.

"No need to be sorry. Have a seat. Eat." Not a command, but an invitation from Catherine, her hand extended to an empty chair beside the baby.

"Thank you."

"No worries," she said as she took her seat on the other side of the table. I eyed the little one, eating with his hands, clumsily lifting chunks of potato to his mouth, dropping more than he ate, the brown sauce of the stew staining his fingers.

"This is Jamie." Darren reached over and rubbed his head, and Jamie leaned into the rub like a dog does a scratch. The room was so quiet that I could hear myself swallow as I used my spoon to push the turnip off to the side.

The night I left, I remember how all the windows were dark except one. The yellow of the hallway night light, put there for the little one, shone out of a second-storey window. I liked him, maybe I had even started to love him. I liked how he would climb onto my lap when I sat watching television, how he curled into me, his thumb in his mouth, his tiny fingers playing with the ends of my hair. He'd arrived only a week before me, the bruises on his tiny legs yellowed before disappearing altogether. He'd begun to smile and laugh, his cheeks filled out, and his eyes became brighter. Someone so small shouldn't have such dark eyes. He was content there with food and warmth, hugs and clean baths. And I suppose I should have been too, but I couldn't let go. It was easy to ignore the feeling when my grandmother was alive, but it was impossible to ignore now. Nothing they could have done would have kept me there. Not even a warm shower and clean bed every night. Instead, I stole money from Catherine's wallet and hitched across two provinces, sleeping in public washrooms and eating out of vending machines, watching myself change in the dirty mirrors of truck stops.

I haven't found my mother. I don't even know where to look. But I did find Gabrielle, with her accent and unfamiliar words, mumbled through her toothless smile. I made the mistake of calling her Gabby once and I was banished from our little alley for two days. Gabrielle with her dark-brown eyes and long silver braid that never seems to look dirty. Gabrielle, who has a box to sleep in. Not any box, but a fridge box, thick, strong and sturdy—immune to the fickle November weather.

There is a small piece of corrugated metal on the top to keep the cardboard from getting soggy and falling in on her. Inside, she has a collection of sleeping bags and all her possessions lined up against the back wall of her box. I took a look at her stuff once, trinkets of no specific value. A small teapot ornament from the Red Rose carton, a music box that didn't work, a swan made of tinfoil. I have no box to sleep in, but she lets me sleep just outside hers, the edges of her roof almost keeping me dry in the rain. It took some time to convince her to let me stay there, without her chasing me away with a pipe she'd stolen from a construction site. She carries the pipe around with her, stuck down the leg of her pants, which makes her limp when she walks.

"In case these men try anything," she says, tapping the pipe under the denim. In the end, she let me stay because of my black hair.

"You look like my daughter, you can stay," she said one night as I wandered into her alley. There were no beds available at the shelter. I felt safe with Gabrielle next to me, asleep inside her cardboard home, her snores loud and constant. So now I have a cold brick wall to lay my sore back against, a sleeping bag with empty garbage bags under it to keep it as dry as possible. During the day, Gabrielle lets me hang my sleeping bag off her roof. Those who are new to the city or to the streets have tried to come into our alley, but Gabrielle chases them away, wielding the pipe over her head and hollering obscenities in at least three different languages.

On particularly bad nights, when my entire body shakes from the cold or my belly howls with hunger, I go to the shelter. I've tried to get Gabrielle to go with me, but she won't, so I bring her coffee and soup, which is cold by the time I get there, but it's still food.

"Bonjour, Melissa, entrez." They always smile when I walk in the door. *"Aimeriez-vous un peu de soupe?"* She is pretty and reminds me of a girl from the new school I went to when I stayed in the house with the blue door. I wish I could remember her name. Maybe it was Amber or Kaitlyn.

"I don't speak French. *Anglais*, please."

"No worry. Do you like some soup?"

"Yes, please."

The food at the shelter is always tepid and always the same. Soup, mashed potatoes with lumps, chicken with gravy, corn and apple pie. I eat fast. I don't like to stick around. Someone always tries to make friends or tries to help. They approach the table with handfuls of pamphlets, optimism brimming from their eyes. They try to get me into "programs." Education, affordable housing, work placement, the church. It's the same thing each time—different people, but the same thing. I prefer to eat alone, in peace. I'm there for food and a bed, not salvation. I sit on my own, scouring the faces, not even sure if I would recognize hers if I saw it. I eavesdrop, hoping to hear her name, and once I did. I followed the man who said it out into the rain, only to see it was the name of his dog, a stray with only one eye and a limp.

The beds here are lined up in a large room, ten to a row. There are iron beds that creak and wooden ones that break. It's comfortable enough, a bed with blankets: real ones, not a sleeping bag that smells of piss and vomit thrown on the floor of the burnt-out house on the rez where everyone goes to party. No one tries to crawl in with me in the middle of the night. Here, they separate the men and the women. The bed in the house with the blue door was comfortable. It was a double and had a duvet.

Everyone who comes to the shelter has to shower before bed. The water isn't hot and it drips from the shower head. There's no shampoo. I stand under the water, the soap refusing to lather in my thick hair. I remember the smell of mint shampoo from my first night at Catherine's house. She let me pick out my own shampoo when the mint one ran out. There were so many choices: melon, green tea and cucumber. All of them named after foods, many of them I'd never even heard of: acai, apricot, pistachios? After my shower, I go back to the narrow bed with the thin, scratchy blankets and flat pillows. I put my dirty clothes back on, and the white, clean socks they leave for us at the end of the bed. Sometimes, when the lights are out and the room is quiet except for the snores and the occasional scream from a nightmare or memory, I wander among the beds. I look into the sleeping faces of the women, looking for my own.

But not tonight. Tonight, I wandered too far from the city centre and didn't get back in time to secure a bed at the shelter. Instead, I take the $4.35 I collected from strangers and buy a coffee and two Timbits. I eat one and shove the other into my pocket for Gabrielle. It wasn't a good day for collection. When it's cold, people bury their faces into their scarves and jackets, their hands enclosed in mittens and gloves. The cold makes it easier for people to ignore me.

Darkness has settled over the city when I finally make my

way back through the noisy streets. The sidewalks are narrow this time of year, the snowbanks packed up against the buildings on one side, the curb on the other, people stepping aside to allow others to pass. No one steps aside for me. When I finally get back to the alley, which is lit by a single light from the back door of the Chinese restaurant, I sit and lean against the brick wall. The familiar sound of cars passing is interrupted by the sound of an animal howling somewhere in the distance. A dog, let out for a piss maybe? Or howling at a raccoon rummaging through the garbage? A coyote too close to the city? A wolf? I shiver. The light barely illuminates Gabrielle, who is hunched over as she paces back and forth across the alleyway. Her pipe sits against the wall, her leg unencumbered. She looks up when she hears me approach. I take the Timbit from my pocket and hand it to her. Sour cream glazed.

"My favourite, *merci*." She pops it into her mouth and chews as best she can with her few remaining teeth before shoving a cigarette butt between her lips. "I am happy you don't smoke, *oui*. It is a terrible thing to do." When she talks, she mixes her French with some English, and I try to make sense of it, picking out words I remember from elementary school French classes. She paces to keep warm, placing her hands on her aging back, forcing herself to stand straight, a new cigarette butt in her fingers, enough for one or two puffs. The smell of tobacco—the sharp and sweet scents mingling together—has always been comforting to me.

"My grandmother smoked and made me promise to never do it." I shiver and pull my knees closer to my chest. The wind has died down, but it's still cold. Bitter cold, the kind that feels like icicles slicing your skin when the wind blows.

"Wise woman, your *grand-mère*." She takes her last puff and lights another butt before rummaging around in the pocket of her jacket, a men's jacket much too big for her tiny frame. "Here, for you."

She hands me a ring, carved of bone or antler, the face of a wolf etched intricately on the face of it. I use the tip of my finger to trace the lines, and shiver.

"It was my daughter's, and you are like her, in your face."

"My grandmother loved wolves." I choke back a sob. I place the ring in the one pocket that zips. I place my hand on the outside of my jacket where a lump has formed, where the ring is safe and protected.

"Like I say before, wise woman." She flings the cigarette

butt across the alleyway. The red sparks disappear into the air as it hits the brick, the smell of tobacco fading. She shuffles off to her box. *"Bonne nuit, Melissa. Bonne nuit."*

"Good night, Gabrielle, and *merci*." I pull the damp sleeping bag up over me, my teeth chattering. The narrowness of the alleyway funnels the wind, its irregularity producing a strange sort of lullaby. My grandmother used to sing lullabies in the language of her mother, a language I never understood but loved.

"YOU ARE SPECIAL," she used to say. "Destined to be great." She'd wave her hands around the room, the wooden panelling peeling away at the top where it met the ceiling. "Promise you will work hard when I'm gone. That you will be great."

"I promise," I said as I stuffed an Oreo into my mouth, not really paying much attention.

"You must promise with your heart, not with your mouth." She snatched the other cookie from my hand and held it out of reach.

"I promise with my heart."

She handed me the cookie.

I can still remember the taste of the tea, no sugar, canned

milk and fresh bread, unleavened, thick and heavy. I smothered the bread in strawberry jam and butter; my grandmother preferred molasses. We sat at the little round table in the kitchen and talked. Or she would talk and I would listen. She'd had grandsons, eight of them, but only one granddaughter. The others were around but never present. Too young and absorbed in creating their own stories, she said, instead of taking the time to listen to hers.

"I have made some arrangements for you." She coughed, a deep phlegmy cough, hard and wet. Her eyes watered as she tried to take a deep breath.

"What you mean?"

"You are a smart girl. You know what I mean. This cancer is coming for me, and I can't let it take me until I know you are going to be okay. This is why I need you to promise with your heart."

"We have lots of time." I shoved another cookie in my mouth.

"We don't. And it's okay. I'm old now, this is not a surprise. There is a woman named Catherine. She's from one of the other communities, I can't remember which one now. My memory is old." She tried to laugh, but another coughing fit racked her thin, frail body.

I didn't say anything, wondering where the conversation was going.

"She was a foster kid back when I was a social worker. She's a good woman and I trust her. She knows what it's like."

"What what's like?"

She didn't answer me. She took a sip of her tea before taking another deep breath. "When I'm gone, she's promised to take care of you. She and her husband. I've arranged it with social services. It's done."

I never stopped to think that my grandmother might actually die. It seemed so strange to me that my life would have to go on without her. But sitting across from her that day, her impending death suddenly became very real.

"You're going to be fine, Nan." I stood to leave the table.

"You need to get ready, my beautiful girl. The world doesn't always do what you want it to."

I wandered down the hall, a sadness settling over me when I heard her whisper, "I will miss you."

When she passed, quietly in her sleep, her hands over her chest and a rosary with a pendant of Saint Kateri entwined in her fingers, I was the only one who truly grieved. The others came and told stories, the Elders sat along the edges of the church basement walls, laughing and sipping tea, but I know that I was the only one who was left with a hole, who felt the void, left alone in a world that turned upside down the moment they lowered her into the ground.

"Hello, Melissa. My name is Kassandra." The social worker wore a grey pantsuit, too big for her small frame. Her hair was thin, stringy and too long, making her look untidy. A gold-plated tag hung loosely from her jacket.

I looked at her out of the corner of my eye. The tea I'd made had gone cold, the thick milk had settled at the top.

"I'm here to help you."

"She's been in the ground for two hours. Couldn't you wait?"

"You're a minor, and I'm very sorry you lost your grand-mother. My primary concern now is that you're taken care of." She moved to sit in my grandmother's chair.

I reached my foot across, grabbing the rung of the chair, pulling it into the table, holding it tight. Kassandra moved to the side, still on her feet.

"I'm so sorry." She stood there watching me until I dropped my foot to the floor, freeing my grandmother's chair. It made the familiar sound of wood scraping along linoleum as she slid it out. "I need you to get your things together, Melissa. Clothes, personal items. I'm not sure if she told you, but your grandmother made arrangements for you."

I nodded. "She told me."

"Good. I'm glad. It's a nice home, and Catherine and her husband are really good people." She waited for me as I collected my things, everything that meant something to me stuffed into two bags.

I left the posters on the wall, the jewellery box sent from god knows where by my mother the last time I heard from her. It had a pink ballerina and used to play music until I broke it when she didn't come back as promised. I threw my clothes into a black garbage bag and grabbed the quilt off my grand-mother's bed before taking one last look around. Her chair, the blanket she draped over her legs when she got a chill, her knitting basket beside it, an unfinished cup of tea, days old now. The last thing I grabbed was the envelope that sat on top of the fridge.

Kassandra's car smelled like imitation pine, the green felt tree dangling from the rear-view mirror as we backed out of the driveway. It swayed back and forth and blocked my view of the house. I sat quietly in the back as Kassandra talked and watched as the street lights came on in sequence. Back at home, the street lights were sketchy at best. One worked for every three that didn't, shot out by guns or burnt-out bulbs too expensive to replace. The light above the blue door came on when we turned into the driveway.

For something so recent, the memory of my grandmother fades more and more each day I'm out here. Most of the time, I can occupy myself with surviving and don't have to think about anything, but when I'm tired and my eyes begin to close, my mind refuses to listen. The only good thing about exhaustion is that I no longer have to think about how to get to sleep; my body takes over for me. The cold becomes secondary to the need for sleep. It softens my muscles, closes my eyes and for a moment tricks me into believing that I'm warm. The memories curl away like the smoke from a cigarette. I close my eyes, my chattering teeth surrender, I pull my knees tight to my chest and listen to the comforting sounds of Gabrielle's snores.

"Wake up."

The voice must be in my dream since I can't feel the cold that seeps under the clothes when you wake up on the concrete.

"Wake up and open your eyes," the voice growls at me.

I open my eyes, the tiny beads of ice that have frozen to my eyelashes breaking and falling.

"Why are you here? Why are you dirty and cold?"

My eyes are tired and take time to adjust to being awake. The air doesn't smell like the trash that constantly lingers in the alleyway. Instead, it smells like the ocean, salty and clean. My head feels heavy, but I lift it toward the sky to take in the sudden heat. I can feel my toes and fingers begin to tingle with warmth. When my eyes finally focus, the clouds that had blanketed the sky when I went to sleep have vanished. A host of tiny stars and a full moon illuminate the concrete and brick. I feel a warmth that until now has been the sole dominion of the sun.

"Grandmother is sending warmth for you."

The smile that had been creeping across my lips disappears as I lower my head and see it standing there in front of me. The wolf has fur thick, glossy and smooth, a soft blend of greys and whites. It stares at me, its head slightly cocked to the side, its black eyes affable yet curious. I can feel the sudden pounding of my heart as the blood pulses in my neck, my cheeks, every part of me flushed with fear. I push my body closer against the wall, sweat beading on my forehead. I survey the alley, careful not to take my eyes fully away from the creature in front of me. I am very aware of being alone. I can still hear Gabrielle snoring. I could call out, but I don't.

"Look at me." A wolf, in this city of concrete, skyscrapers, cars, taxis, trains and people. I must be dreaming, there is no other explanation. Or maybe I'm dead.

"I'm dreaming. Wolves don't talk." I look around for something that will wake me. The wolf gives me a dismissive sniff and continues to look at me, unblinking.

"I've been asked to visit you."

The wolf stretches like a cat after a nap, and then walks toward me. I can feel its breath on my face.

"You have been given a gift, and you promised that you would not waste it. Do you remember?" The wolf sits down in front of me, waiting. "You promised to be more than this. Do you remember?"

"I remember." The words stick in the back of my throat. The face of my grandmother, glancing over her glasses, teacup in hand, flashes in the black eyes of the wolf.

"Then tell me why you are here."

"I don't . . . I don't know? My mother." I wipe my nose with the corner of the sleeping bag.

"Your mother?"

"Her last letter." I reach into the bottom of the sleeping bag, pulling out the envelope, holding it up.

"She is not here."

"I just hoped . . ."

"Is this the life you promised?"

The snores of Gabrielle finally break into the quiet as she struggles to get her breath.

"I need you to go home."

"I don't have a home."

"Go back to the house with the blue door. Those are the people who will care for you."

"But . . ."

"Go home, Melissa. Your grandmother made the best choice for you." The wolf takes a breath, irritated. "And the little one misses you."

"I don't understand."

"You're not meant to understand. You're meant to be a child. Now go home."

THE SUN IS BRIGHT when I open my eyes. I'm lying on my back on the cold pavement, stiff from the cold and the concrete. The soft warmth of the moon is long gone. The smell of garbage is back in my nose. There are people all around, bending over me, staring at me. Someone has placed a thick grey blanket over me, and a man is holding my wrist, counting my heartbeats through my skin. The sun breaks through the cold, and I squint to see who is around me.

"What's going on? Where's Gabrielle? Gabrielle!" I call out for her, but there is only the din of police and paramedics. My legs are weak when I try to stand. I fall, landing hard on the cold concrete. Someone is cooing soothing words that I don't understand. I'm too weak to protest when they secure me to a long yellow board and place me in one of the two ambulances. I try to see out the back doors.

"Where is Gabrielle?" I want to shout, but the cold has left my throat dry. The other ambulance slowly begins to pull away. The lights don't flash, and the siren is mute. One of the police officers pokes his head in to talk to me.

"She's gone, sweetheart. I am surprised you survived. Coldest night in twelve years, so they say. You seem okay, but we're going to take you to the hospital and get you checked out just to make sure. Get you a hot meal, and call your folks." His accent is subtle, and his words are kind.

"Where are you taking her?" I see the other ambulance turn a corner and disappear.

"We will take good care of her for you. I promise."

The police officer nods and closes the door, keeping the heat in and the sounds of the city out. The paramedic sits beside me, two fingers on my wrist. I let my body go, let my muscles relax, unclench my jaw and let my mouth fall open, staring at the grooved ceiling of the ambulance. My fingers, clasped tight, loosen and the ring falls to the floor. I try to sit, but the paramedic gently pushes me back. He bends down and places the ring back in my hand.

"I'd like to go home, please," I say, as I close my hands around the ring.

THE BIRTHING TREE

My mother died pushing me into this world. Her blood spread out on the ground around her, the dirt a coppery red and the smell of lightning on the air. I don't know if I saw her face or if she saw mine. Only that, by the first crack of thunder, she was gone.

It isn't a particularly nice tree, the one where my mother died. The roots exposed like ugly veins popping out of the earth. It leans over, some of the heavier branches touching the top of the pond. When the seasons change, the tree doesn't. The leaves just sit on top of the water or fall to the ground, brown and slippery. But none of that matters, Grandmother tells me, because this tree holds our stories. This tree presides over our entry into this world. It makes mothers out of women and fathers out of men. No one else can see it, but I swear, when the sun is creeping through the branches and kissing the ground, the roots glow red.

"This year, you're going to start helping me welcome the babies. Your mother caught a few babies before she crossed over. Now it's your turn."

I stopped and held my teacup close to my lips as the steam blurred my vision. She smiled and nodded before she got up to investigate a noise. I sat for only a minute before I followed, leaving my tea on the table as the leaves sank to the bottom. The cat jumped up and sniffed the crumbs of my abandoned bread before it licked off the butter.

"And it looks like you won't have to wait too long for your first."

Through the small window that sits over the sink, I saw Sally as she wandered across the field, one baby on her back and the other on her hip. I grabbed the bucket and rushed out the back door to fetch water. It was September, but still hot for a woman so big with child.

"A third. Let's hope she gets a girl this time," Grandmother muttered under her breath.

The water sloshed out of the bucket when I placed it on

the ground, too abruptly, in my rush to greet Sally. She was seated now. Grandmother was crouched behind her, rubbing her back. The younger boy slept under a blanket, held up with two sticks, draped over the top to keep the sun off. His birthmark, so red last summer when he rushed into the world, was faded, a small mark just below his right eye. His brother sat at his mother's side, his chin nearly touching his chest as he struggled to stay awake, curious about his new surroundings. I had watched my grandmother guide both of them into the world.

"You look well, Sally." I dipped her cup into the bucket and handed it to her.

"Yes, well enough, I suppose, since I'm having another, and soon." She held the cup to the older boy's lips and he took a sip, his eyes parting only long enough to swallow. "And your grandmother tells me that you will be helping me welcome this one into the world." She smiled at me, none of the fear I felt in my belly showing on her face. "I will try my best not to rush it like last time." She reached over and rubbed the tummy of the sleeping boy.

"Sally, since you're the first to arrive, why don't you sleep inside with us. Be a shame to have you sleeping on the ground, out here all on your own." My grandmother took the older boy and I grabbed her supplies, those I could carry, and they came inside with us. I gave them my bed and I slept with my grandmother until Big Ben arrived to set up their own tent. Over the next few days the field beside our house filled with tents, small fires, friends and family members who hadn't seen one another since the last harvest. Laughter and shouts of welcome echoed off the trees that bordered the small field. My ugly cousin with short, cropped hair because of the lice, and teeth already beginning to colour with rot, arrived with my auntie. He walked by me smirking.

"Half-breed," he sneered.

His mother gave him a swat on the head. "You shut your mouth. You pay no attention to him, Aliet, he's full of piss and vinegar, this one. Just like his daddy." My uncle was an ass, that's what Grandmother called him, swearing me to secrecy about it.

Half-breed. I let the word roll around in my head, repeating it over and over in clenched whispers.

"Sally, am I a half-breed?"

She looked up as I sat down across from her, the baby asleep on her lap. "Good God, Aliet, where did you learn that? You are exactly what the ancestors had in mind, and I won't hear another word about it."

The older boy plopped himself on my lap and began using my hands to clap. The word and all it implied vanished off my tongue and slipped out of my mind.

As the sun began to sink and I waited for Grandmother to call my name to come for supper, Big Ben arrived. He wandered through the rows of tents, stopping to greet friends and share a laugh. He'd been out on a fishing boat, the ones that go out for days at a time, and so arrived late. Sally didn't like him fishing, but it brought in good money.

"If he keeps putting these babies in me, he's going to have to spend a lot more time at sea. Gotta feed them all now." She laughed at her own joke as he bent down to kiss her on the forehead.

"It's good to see you, Aliet. I swear, you'll be as tall as me this time next year."

He still smelled of salt water. I blushed.

I liked Big Ben. He was light skinned like me and he always brought me a penny. He turned my small, freckled hand over and placed the penny in my palm before closing my fingers around it.

"Now don't spend it all in one place, Aliet," he said, chuckling to himself.

With each new penny, I tried to memorize the details of his hand. The broken lines, the shape of his nails, an odd-shaped freckle like the one that sat above my pinky finger on my right hand. Later, I sat on my small bed and tried to remember every detail, comparing them to mine, trying to find a likeness.

My ugly cousin never got a penny. No one liked him much except his mother, and even that I still don't believe with my whole heart. But that day, he saw me get one.

"Big Ben isn't your father, you know. I think it's the man who buys our baskets, the one with the curly hair and missing thumb."

He snuck up on me as I was leaving Sally and Big Ben, the penny still clutched in my hand. I turned so fast, he was surprised, and even more so when I punched him square in the mouth, sending his head flying backwards. He stumbled but didn't fall, blood dripping down his chin, shock on his face. My knuckle was split, a cut the size of his two front teeth, and my own blood seeped in between the clenched fingers of my fist. I wasn't even sorry I did it. He wiped his hands on his pants, turned and walked away. He never did tell Grandmother. I don't know what he told my aunt and uncle, but I never got in trouble. Sally and Big Ben pretended they hadn't seen a thing.

"Get that cleaned up, Aliet," was all Sally said.

THAT EVENING, my hand wrapped tightly with a homemade bandage and smelling of iodine, I walked the fields, moving to avoid playing children, breathing in the smell of bread fried in pork fat over an open fire, waiting for the first stories to be told over firelight, the first songs to be sung. But it wasn't the food or the stories I was interested in, it was the faces.

I don't know what she looked like, my mother. I've never seen a photo. No one's ever told me how dark her hair was and if it went light under the sun the way mine does in summer. If her mouth was small or her smile wide. Was her nose tiny? Were her eyes brown? Maybe they were dark green like mine. Maybe she had the same gold flecks that everyone admired. The green a result, my grandmother said, of an Irishman or a Scotsman, generations ago. The gold, a gift from God. So, I looked here, among these people who were my people.

But I always settled on Big Ben.

"Kiju, who's my father?"

She turned to face me as I entered the kitchen, the last of the summer sun throwing shadows, casting her in half-light.

"I don't know. She never said."

"You think it could be Big Ben?" I asked.

"I suppose. They were friendly. He was a couple years younger, only sixteen, I think, when you came around. But Ben's a good man. If he knew you were his kid, he'd claim you."

"Maybe she never told him."

"Where is all this coming from? Who you been talking to?"

"No one. Just that everyone else has a father but me. I don't have a mother or a father. Just think it's a bit unfair, that's all. And Ben's light like me."

"His father was Acadian, died of a fever before he was born." She shooed the cat off the counter with her soapy hands. "His mother could say the Lord's Prayer in French and thought she was better than the rest of us because of it." She rolled her eyes and threw me a smile. "And don't you worry, Aliet, you got me. Now get up here and start drying these dishes. You're not bringing up something like that just to get out of doing your chores." She lifted her hand out of the dishwater and blew a soapy pile of bubbles into my hair and laughed.

The next evening, I was taking Sally the tea that would thicken her body for childbirth when I saw her lying on her side, breathing as I'd seen Mr. Anderson's cows do when a calf was about to be born. Big Ben was making his way through the tents, just back from a hot day in the potato fields.

Sally looked up at me and whispered, "I'm ready to go."

I stood frozen to the ground.

"Aliet, stop looking so worried. We're all the same, girl, all animals. We birth the same and die the same. This is as natural a thing as the sun coming up in the morning. Besides, you watched the other two being born."

I ran back to the house and Grandmother and I gathered the herbs used for guiding babies into the world, a small kettle, a metal cup and a new hide to wrap the baby in, softened over the winter.

When I returned, Sally was on her feet. Big Ben was gently handing her over to the women who'd come to help. He took the two boys, kissed Sally and disappeared to his brothers' fire. The women began to hum, their deep, rumbling voices lifting Sally out of the pain. The path to the tree wasn't long, a five-minute walk when there wasn't a baby trying to be born. We got to the tree as the moon was rising, and Sally found herself a comfortable spot between two large roots, one arm draped over each root, embracing the tree.

I lit the fire while Grandmother checked on the position of the baby. "Head first, Sally, nothing to worry about. Aliet's getting some tea ready that's going to help you keep your strength. For now, just hum along with us."

I gathered some water from the pond and placed a handful of white spruce needles in to steep, humming along to the same song we welcomed each baby with. I loved the song, not only because it welcomed babies into the world but because it was our song, the men didn't know it, it belonged only to us.

Grandmother waved me over to her, her hands resting on Sally's thighs. The light from the lantern flickered, muting the pain on Sally's face.

"Are you ready, Aliet?"

I couldn't seem to speak and I felt all my breath leaving my body. I dropped to my knees and Grandmother took my hands and placed them on the insides of Sally's thighs. Sally looked down and smiled, nodding her head.

"Don't worry, Aliet, I trust you."

I took a deep breath and looked behind me to see my grandmother stirring the tea. I took one last look into the mass of leaves to see the sliver of moon shining through.

The baby was born easy, just like the other two. Two strong pushes and his head slipped out. I grabbed it, gently turned it, to help Sally out a bit. The humming turned into song.

"One more, Sally, one more and we should be good."

She took a deep breath and the women sang louder. Sally clenched her teeth and pushed and the baby came out in a rush of fluid, clear and scented of salt water. I sat back for just a second to gaze at this little human I had helped guide into the world. Another boy, his head full of black hair, his face all squished. He cried his first cry as I placed him on Sally's chest, my hands and arms wet with birth. The song was over. I reached to grab the twine and tied off the cord, cutting it with Grandmother's knife and setting it aside. Sally would want to take it home and bury it with the others to remind her children where their home will always be. The ground darkened where he entered the world, Sally's blood joining the blood of our women, the blood of my own mother.

She cooed and kissed his wet head, whispering to him.

"Aliet, clean up now and get the tea ready."

Grandmother's voice snapped me out of my daze as she

took the baby from Sally and washed him with water that smelled of spruce before wrapping him in soft leather and placing him at his mother's breast. I washed my hands in the remaining water before returning it to the earth, and put a fresh kettle on to boil. The women started to leave, returning to their own families. One of them would tell Big Ben to come, now that the song was over and the baby was here. Sally pulled the leather hide away so I could see his face. Even through the cloudy eyes of a newborn, and in the dim light of a lantern, I could see the fleck of gold in his dark-green eyes.

ANOTHER DEAD INDIAN

"Just another dead Indian," I hear him mutter under his breath as he turns and walks down the stairs, swinging his keys on his finger. "An accident," he calls over his shoulder. "No investigation needed." As the door to the police cruiser shuts, my mother, who's been so quiet and still, collapses, her hand still gripping the metal handle of the screen door.

"Mom, let me help you up." I reach under her arms and lift her off the floor. She is a small woman, a full head shorter than me, but she is heavy with unexpected grief. "Mom, you need to let go." I unwrap her hand from the door handle and take the carrot she was peeling from the other, placing it on the shelf above our heads, the one with knitted hats and assorted mismatched mittens.

Her legs shake and her walk is unsteady as she leans against me. We make our way to her chair, the one by the big window, the one where she sits and watches the birds at the bird feeder. Where she curses the squirrels for stealing her seeds. She slumps over, the tears routing through the wrinkles just beginning to deepen with her fifty-two years.

"Mom, who's dead? What accident?"

She looks up at me, her middle son, my hair dishevelled from sleep.

"Rufus," she chokes. Saying his name seems to make the grief that much harder.

"I'll make some tea."

She nods and turns back to the window. It's not yet noon, but the kitchen has been alive for hours. When I got home from my night shift at the mill, she was already making bread, humming songs that I've been listening to since I was small but will never know the names of.

"Mornin', Ma."

"Mornin', my boy."

I grabbed a cookie, careful to avoid the piece of bread she keeps in the jar so the cookies stay soft, and headed down the hall to bed.

"Chicken for dinner," she hollered after me.

"Can't wait."

And now I stand here, my hands empty and my mother crying in the other room. The potatoes are peeled and sitting in a pot of water, enough to feed seven. A chicken is roasting in the oven and a pile of carrot shavings sits abandoned, beginning to brown and curl. Fresh bread sits on the side counter, cooling. On any other day, my eyes on the kettle, my body leaning against the counter, my fingers tapping the side of the mug impatiently, she would tell me that a watched pot never boils. Today, my eyes on the steam but my mind a million miles away, I create pictures of my uncle Rufus in my mind. I jump when the kettle whistles and drop the tiny teacup on the floor, where it shatters. My mother stops sobbing in the other room.

"Don't worry, Mom, just a broken glass." I pour her tea into a blue cup, a country scene on it, one of the collectors' teacups from the gas stations on the other side of the border that Dad picks up for her when he's on the road. Red Rose, no milk, no sugar, steeped long enough to leave a dry bitterness on the tongue.

"Mom, your tea." My breath gets caught in my throat when she looks at me, her eyes red and wet. I've never seen my mother cry like this. Tears of joy, of course: when I graduated high school, when my brother and his wife gave her a grand-child, a boy named John. But never tears of grief.

"He was all the family I had left." She turns to face the window again, the steaming cup cradled in her hands. "I don't mean you guys." She looks back at me, panic mixed with grief.

"I know." I sit on the floor beside her chair, my hand on her lap, open, waiting for hers, while she sips her tea and stares at the clouds, greying around the edges, promising rain. Her parents were gone before she was even married. And now her only brother, dead.

"The rain will be good. Be good for the garden." She sighs as she watches a blue jay hop his way over to the feeder. "He was a good fisherman and a great swimmer . . ."

The end of her sentence trails off into a whisper.

I look at the clock hanging on the wall. Ten hours until my father calls, if he calls. Sometimes he can't find a phone along the interstate. I'm relieved when the screen door opens and I hear my brother's backpack hit the floor in the front porch.

"I skipped out. It was track and field day anyway. Hope that's okay, Mom." He walks into the room, pulling his sweater up over his head. It's that time of year when the cold sticks around for the morning but the heat takes over in the afternoon, only for the cold to return again in the evening, leaving everyone perpetually unsure how to dress.

"What's going on?" His eyes move from Mom to me and back again. Mom doesn't look away from the blue jay, pecking at the seeds, strewing them on the ground. "Mom."

No response. He stands frozen, his shirt pulled off over his head, hanging from hidden hands. I gesture for him to come over and he pulls the sweater back up over his head to cover his bare chest.

"Mom, I'm going to town to see what happened," I say, standing up. "Uncle Rufus is dead," I whisper in my brother's ear, as if saying it too loudly will somehow make it worse.

Her shoulders heave, the way a wave does just before crashing into land, and the tears start again. But she never looks away from the blue jay, tea in one hand, my brother's hand in the other.

The clouds that had begun to assemble earlier move faster now, the grey creeping from the edges and into the centre. The leaves on the trees rustle, breaking the quiet that comes before a storm, when the birds stop singing and nest their heads in their feathers. The insects, even the ones of early spring, hide away. The stones crunch under my feet as I walk in the middle of the tracks, the rails on either side, rusting and still. I listen for the train, but it's not expected for another hour, plenty of time to get to town. I've only miscalculated once and had to jump off the tracks, rolling down a small embankment, flattening a few small bushes on my way down, the thorns of the purple thistles biting in retaliation. The wind is picking up, but the chill keeps the bugs away. I left in a hurry, without thinking. I don't have a jacket and I still stink from work; wood shavings litter my hair and my T-shirt is wrinkled and slept in. Up ahead, framed by the green pines, I can see the occasional car slow down as it passes over the tracks. I'm almost there.

The police station sits in the middle of town, not five minutes from the train station. It's small and attached to the town hall, the fire station and a small room where they store bodies until the funeral home takes them. That room is rarely used. Most people die at home or at the hospital. Murder around here is almost unheard of. Almost. Together, the different municipal departments form a large U-shaped building surrounded by carefully manicured bushes and flower gardens in the summer. You enter by the front, the door made of thick, dark wood, heavy and far too ornate for such a small town, the scales of justice cruelly carved into the wood. It's just before noon when I get there, and the rain has managed to hold off. The vestibule is dark and cool, windowless and lit by two lights over the reception counter.

"I'd like to talk to someone in the police department." I know them all, of course, everyone does in a small town. But not all of them like those of us who live on the edge of town. They only seem to appreciate us when they need someone to blame for something. A stolen car, a broken window, and they mutter under their breath, *Must be those Indians*. I know a good many white boys from high school who got into far more trouble than we did. But their pale faces put them on the right side of the law, regardless of their crime.

"Take a seat, I'll see if I can find someone to talk to you." The man sits behind a wall of glass and closes the small door that allows him to take change and talk to you. I stand against the wall and wait, watching the clock tick away the minutes. The sunlight on the floor moves over my feet and up the wall, and is disappearing altogether when the mayor walks through.

"James." He nods at me as he leaves for lunch. I nod in return. I painted his house last summer.

The receptionist, the one who likes to flirt with me at dances when she's had a little too much to drink but doesn't see fit to talk to me otherwise, lowers her head and mumbles my name when she sees me, afraid I might learn something from the way she holds her eyes.

I stand and watch as people come and go, some paying their bills, others hanging notices on the community bulletin board. Church dinners and Legion dances. One man, upset at the lack of fish available in the river this spring, demands to see the mayor and I snicker.

It's dusk before someone comes out to speak to me. I'm supposed to be at work at seven for a twelve-hour night shift, but I don't care. I'm not leaving until someone talks to me. I need to be able to tell my mother something when I get home.

"James, what are you doing here?"

It's Jake. I went to school with him. He's nice enough and always has been. We played on the baseball team together, developing that all-important relationship between a pitcher and his catcher.

"My uncle's dead and I want to know how."

"Yeah, I heard about that. Sorry, man." He shifts from one foot to the other, fascinated by something on the floor. "You been waiting long?"

"Since noon."

"Shit, man, I just came on."

"So, how is it that my uncle ended up dead?" I push myself off the wall I was leaning against and stand up straight. I have almost a foot on him, his thin shoulders no match for the ones I've built up hauling logs at the mill. The dim lights throw shadows and I know I look intimidating. But I don't care.

"You're a little excited there, James. Just take a seat and calm down a minute."

"I've had hours to calm down. Now I need you to tell me what happened to my uncle."

Jake moves to sit but, seeing that I have no intention, stands back up, too quickly, and almost loses his balance. I reach over and catch him by the arm, steadying him.

"Drowned, from what I hear. Out fishing on the lake. They found his boat overturned and his body on the beach."

He won't look at me.

"Drowned?"

"Drowned."

Behind him, someone on the other side of the glass turns off the lights inside the offices.

"I want to see him. I want to see my uncle, Jake."

He shifts his weight from one foot to the other again. His discomfort is rhythmic.

"I'm not leaving until I see my uncle."

The janitor brushes past us, placing his hand on the brim of his hat as he walks out the door. "You lock up, Jake?"

"I will. I'm staying anyhow. On duty. Just gotta get James here to head on home."

The janitor eyes me, wondering if he should stay or go. He decides to leave and the door closes heavy behind him.

"Go out the back, under the big spruce, there's a back door. Make sure no one sees ya. Maybe walk around the block once, in case any busybodies are watching. By now they all know you're in town. And they'll be watching to make sure you leave."

"So, you knew I was here all afternoon but said you didn't. Very Christian of you to leave me out here."

"It's complicated, James."

"Seems simple to me. My uncle is dead. A man who could lead a canoe to land in a hurricane. A man who could swim clear across Greenfield Lake in November. But he's dead, drowned. I come for answers, and no one wants to give them to me."

"I'm trying to help you. Just do what I told ya."

"If you're not here when I get back from my loop around the block, I have no problem coming to your house and waiting until you let me see my uncle."

The door closes behind me and I hear the click of the lock falling into place. Tiny specks of rain dot the sidewalk. The cool drops feel good on my warm face. I turn left toward the train tracks, making sure anyone watching thinks I'm leaving town. The block is a short one; one road has a cemetery on each side, one has the school, and the others are littered with houses—the nice kind where the mayor lives, big verandahs and high windows.

I stop just before the wooden door, searching the windows of the houses across the road once more, the pale-yellow light filtered through the curtains, looking for the faces of the curious, but there are none I can see. I make my way around the side of the building and duck behind the spruce to get to the back door. Jake meets me there, the small, bald light bulb making shadows out of both of us.

"Now, James, I just need you to know that I had nothing to do with the telling of the story. You need to trust me on that." He stands in front of me in the dim light from the hallway, blocking my way.

I nod and he leads me down a hall to a metal door. Through a small window I can see my uncle, still clothed, lying on a table.

"I'd like to tell you to take your time, but the funeral home will be by any time now to take him." Jake continues down the hall and through a door, leaving me alone.

I've never been alone with a dead person. Until this moment, I've only ever seen one, a great-aunt I barely knew, and it was so long ago, I can't even remember what she looked like. And she died peacefully in her sleep, a heart attack at seventy-two. This is different, this is someone I ate breakfast with just three days ago, sitting at the table, he was spreading too much butter on his toast.

The metal door scrapes against the cement floor as the cold rushes past me and into the hall. My legs feel weak and my feet are glued to the floor. I breathe deep and go in. The door closes behind me with a swoosh. I take his hand. Shaken by how cold it is, I pull my hands away and take a minute to compose myself. His lips are blue and his face is bloated. They've closed his eyes, a small mercy. He barely resembles the uncle who could cut down a birch tree in less than a minute, who could make my mother smile just by walking into the room.

His wrists are marked with dark-purple indentations, the flesh flayed at the edges. I use my finger to trace the ugly lines. The cold of the room has left his clothes in a semi-frozen state, white patches on his breast pocket, on his right knee. His feet haven't fallen to the side but instead stick straight up, his boots still on. They hadn't gotten around to removing the fishing twine from his ankles. It's wound tight. I reach between his feet, feeling the tautness of the nylon. It barely budges. This is something I was never meant to see.

Jake knocks on the other side of the steel door and waves for me through the small window.

"Drowned?" I say as I exit the room. The door swings back and hits the brick wall behind it.

"Drowned. That's what they told the newspaper."

"And what they told my mother. What do you think I should tell her now, Jake?"

"Drowned, James. No need to get her all worked up."

"Drowned. Just the same way those two Black men drowned three summers ago?"

Jake's face goes red, but he stays silent. I wait. I have nowhere to be but here.

"Same lake, too."

"There's nothing I can do, James. You know that. You know it as well as me. Better, even."

"Anyone else out on that lake yesterday?"

"I don't know. I'm being honest, I don't know."

"Who found him? After he drowned."

The building is quiet; only the tree branches tapping the windows make a sound. Out of the corner of my eye I watch a mouse run from one corner of the hallway and squeeze its tiny body under a door. Jake turns to walk down the hall and I grab his arm.

"Come on, come down to the office. It's just me in right now. Come and have a drink."

The windows are tall and look out onto a courtyard between the fire station and the police station. I can see that the wind is up, leaves and small twigs forming miniature tornadoes in the corners of the building. I let go of his arm and follow.

Jake's desk is one of three lined up against a wall, nothing remarkable about it. A typewriter and some notepads lie strewn around. A coffee cup, half-full, sits too close to the edge and I reach over and move it so it won't fall. Aside from us and I imagine a few more mice, no one else is in the building. Jake reaches down and opens a drawer, takes out a bottle of something brown, no label, and pours two drinks into empty coffee mugs, stolen from the other desks. I take a sip.

"Homemade?" I wince and it burns its way down to my belly.

Jake nods and drinks his in one gulp. He pours himself another.

"Those brothers. Lionel and whatshisname. They found him."

"Same as those other men." I take another sip, feeling it all the way down.

"Yup."

"Nothing weird about that?"

"Everything weird about that, and you know it. Why you trying to give me a hard time?" He takes his second drink, tipping it up and swallowing hard.

"My uncle is dead and my mother is grieving and I'm giving you a hard time?" I know Jake can't do anything, just as I know I can't do anything. But I need answers. I'm biding my time, trying to think of something to say to my mother. "I gotta tell my mother something, Jake."

"Just easier if you tell her he drowned."

"Just another dead Indian, eh, Jake?"

"I didn't say that."

Both of us turn and look out the window on the other side of the room, across from the line of desks, as the rain begins to fall in earnest, sliding down the glass.

"I gotta go. Thanks for the drink."

"Please don't thank me."

The sky is dark now, the grey has taken over completely, the storm and the night fighting each other for space. The leaves, so vocal in their opposition to the weather earlier in the day, have gone quiet, bending into themselves in an act of self-preservation. The raindrops are fat and heavy, and I swear I can hear them hit the ground one by one. I try to count them as I wait for the roar of the train to pass. By the time the train is nothing but a blur in the distance, the rain is falling in sheets. I start to walk, trying my best to figure out what I'm going to say to my mother.

SWEETGRASS

Mother's feet sink into the mud, the difference between flesh and earth nearly impossible to distinguish. The mud hugs her as if welcoming a long-lost sister. I bend and trace a circle around her ankle where the mud and my mother meet. My dress is muddied and Mother's soft hand rests on my head.

"Epit'jij, pay attention to your grandmother. Come, my girl."

I look over as she puts her hand in the water, grabbing the bottom of the stalk, using the flint blade, gifted by Naku'set but shaped by my father, to cut the stalks from the earth.

The sun is just coming up over the water; the water fairies are dancing, welcoming the sunrise. The clouds are the colour of cold hands turning warm again. It's too early even for the birds. Grandmother and Mother hum in unison, soft and quiet. It's a song I don't know, but Mother assures me that it's simply hiding away in my heart, waiting for the right time.

We travelled yesterday from the camp, leaving my father behind with the four younger children. They waved as we ducked into the woods, finding the river and following it to the ocean. We stayed awake praying to the full moon, our fingers, toes and bellies full of the water she gave us. Only when the sun began to sneak above the line where water meets the sky did Grandmother open her eyes and gesture for us to collect our gathering tools and follow her.

Grandmother knows the best places to pick sweetgrass. "Where the water that tastes like tears meets the water that tastes like the river. This is where Kisu'lkw placed the most fragrant and sweetest," she whispers. I think she knows that if we speak too loudly, the pink of the sky will shatter. Mother often says that I am like my grandmother.

Mother moves forward, her feet sinking gently into the earth again. I follow and enjoy the cool, soft mud. I stop to wiggle my toes, the little beads of mud sputtering away to rejoin the rest of the wet earth. Mother uses her hand to push the tall grass to the side, allowing us to move effortlessly until she stops, holding the grass away from me in the direction of the sun. She moves her hand up the green stalks as they fall away until only the greenest remain, glowing in the early morning light. The sweet smell reaches my nose and I breathe in.

"This is how you know it's the hair of the great mother, epit'jij. It will glow."

Grandmother moves off, collecting more in the silence of the dawn, while Mother shows me how to cut the grass. Later, when it's dried and we are home among our family, we will braid it as we do our own hair. As I reach beneath the cool water of morning and grasp my first stalk, I begin to hum softly.

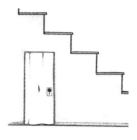

IN THE NAME OF GOD

The question doesn't seem dangerous. It seems harmless, and I even ask it in English. But Sister Agnus doesn't think it's so harmless. Her face turns purple like the radish we grow in the gardens but never get to eat.

"Matthew, come here. Now."

White spittle forms in the corners of her mouth as I make my way to the front. Her mouth turns down at the edges and the wrinkles around them deepen. When she's angry like this, Thomas says you could drive a tractor through them. The old wooden desks are lined up in rows, the girls on one side, the boys on the other. Their tops are still shiny from the cleaning they got a couple of weeks ago, before the government inspectors came. No one breathes as I make my way down the aisle, my hands at my side, suddenly heavy. I stop and focus my eyes on the wooden floor and force my heavy hands to come together in front of me. The room is so quiet, I can hear my own breathing when she raises her hand and brings the ruler down on the top of my head. I try not to wince, but I know she sees me squeeze my eyes shut and purse my lips together. Weakness is a sin for Sister Agnus, and the ruler comes down a second time. I feel the warmth of the blood, but I don't dare reach up to check. This time I hold in my pain, pushing air against the inside of my belly to keep my face straight. She sends Muriel to fetch Father Jacob.

"You just stay quiet and do as they ask. Don't make trouble and it'll be fine," my mother said to me the day she dropped us off at the front door. "There's food here. Remember that, there's food here. You need to eat." She reached down and straightened my socks. "Your father would want you to have food." She reached over and did the same to my sister, pulling her socks up. They had white ruffles, a gift from the church.

"He'd be okay with this. He'd want you to have food." She wouldn't look up, wouldn't look at us when she spoke to us.

"He would approve, I know he would." She used the same voice that she used when she was trying to convince us of something we didn't want to believe, like onions are tasty and that eating carrots, when we used to have carrots, would help us see better.

Sister Agnus and Father Jacob stood on either side of the imposing doors, two black towers, grim-faced and still.

My stomach growled and betrayed me. I wrapped my arms around my thin waist as I tried to hold in the sound. It'd been two days since food passed through our lips. My mother had lost her job cleaning the diner at night because she took three pieces of apple pie, stale and destined for the trash but still sweet. They told her she was stealing. If she'd just waited until they threw it in the trash, it would have been okay.

"I love you," she whispered.

The hem of my sister's dress fluttered in the breeze created by my mother's hurried exit. She rushed down the stairs, across the lawn and through a small opening in the trees, and was gone before the sensation of the kiss she left on my cheek had time to fade. We didn't even have time to consider that she wasn't staying, that we were being left behind. A heavy hand on my shoulder turned me toward the door and into the foyer. The same hand turned me to the right. A different hand turned my sister to the left. I turned to see her grab the door frame. She held on tight, not moving. Her eyes were wide and damp with tears.

"We just have to be good for a while. She'll come back."

Her lips had turned down, her eyes wide and brimming, the tears sitting on the edges, waiting to fall.

"Trust me."

She nodded as her small brown hands softly released the door, a half-hearted attempt at a smile before the door closed and she was gone.

Father Jacob bent down, his other hand resting on my other shoulder. They felt warm but heavy, as though I was being pushed into the earth. I looked down to make sure my feet still stood on the solid wood floor.

"Thank you for that, Matthew. You must have said something very comforting to your sister. But we don't speak like that here. We speak English and Latin only. Do you understand me? I know you speak English."

I nodded. My father, before a bullet in a farmer's field somewhere in a place called France killed him, spoke their language to us. Mother insisted on her own. I nodded and he stood tall, his thin frame towering over me, his cassock billowing through the door that separated the boys from the girls.

I WAS GOOD. For an entire year, I'd been good. I listened to my mother, did what she said to do. I said what they wanted me to say, learned what they wanted me to learn, prayed the way they wanted me to pray and ate the food she wanted me to eat. But Thomas, the boy who spent the most time in the cupboard, warned me it would happen.

"Eventually, we all disappoint them. The boys more than the girls. They go easier on the girls," he said. The girls had to spend their time in the office with Father Jacob, reading Scripture on their knees. But the boys, we got the cupboard.

I stand at the front of the room as the other students look down at their hands or at the floor. Muriel comes rushing back through the door, the soles of her tattered shoes scraping the floor. She takes her seat and lowers her eyes, just like the others. None of them will look at me. I can feel the little trail of blood warming the side of my head and running down behind my ear, but I don't want to reach up and wipe it, afraid it would invoke a third hit to my already tender head. Sister Agnus goes to the door, where she and Father Jacob talk, discussing my crime in hushed whispers and disappointed glances. The clock ticks behind me and I start to count the seconds, quietly inside my head.

"Matthew, follow me." Sister Agnus, her hands folded in front of her, *tsk*s at me through her teeth when I pass through the door and follow Father Jacob down the hall, my shorter legs trying to keep pace. Father Jacob is always in a hurry to punish. I think he enjoys it. I find it hard to keep up without running, but running isn't permitted. Just past the bathroom, the one with running water and a toilet that flushes, used only by the teachers, he turns, grabs my arm and drags me down the long hallway. It feels as if he's going to pull my arm right off my body.

We head toward the main doors, the same ones I came in through over a year ago, and I can see the snow falling heavy and thick through the narrow windows that frame the large wooden doors. For an instant I think he is going to open the doors and throw me out into the cold. But instead, he turns and we head down the dark hall to the kitchen. The white of the snow is still in my eyes, making the darkness of the hall- way all the more menacing. The dim lights that hang from the ceiling throw sinister shadows on the paintings of saints and their gruesome deaths. Saint Catherine and her wheel, Saint Bartholomew, holding his own skin, Saint Stephen, a stone in his hand.

"I'm sorry, Father Jacob. I really am. I didn't mean to. I was just wondering." I know where he's taking me, and I don't want to go.

"You'll have plenty of time to consider your words."

The kitchen air is warm and still smells of boiled oats from breakfast. At Christmas they give us strawberry jam and fresh, warm milk for our oats, but on every other day of the year they give us salt.

There is a pain in my belly. It's moved there from my chest since we left the classroom. I don't like the dark, and I hate small spaces. Thomas told us about the cupboard. He's been in there twice now since I've been here. Muriel says he's been here longer than anyone can remember. They keep him because he is strong and simple. He's obedient, but has a quick temper that is as unpredictable as a lightning strike. He's good for chores, but every once in a while they have to put him in the cupboard. No one knows how many times and he says he can't remember.

Thomas isn't a bad person; he just doesn't understand things the way the rest of us do. The other kids, in whispers after the prayers are recited and the light is turned out, say that his mother died when he was born and he didn't breathe for a whole ten minutes. They'd given up on him and placed him in a box by the fire. Then he just started wailing, and he wailed until someone dropped him off at the steps one day with a note scribbled in barely understandable English. Now he sometimes says and does things that get him into trouble.

We all wonder what's under Sister Agnus's habit. I always imagined that she hid a smaller Sister Agnus under there, one that whispered in her ear, telling her when we were misbehaving. My mother always told me I had the mind of a storyteller. Muriel thinks that she has a long black braid darker than a moonless night, and Thomas thinks she might be bald like his grandfather. None but Thomas dared ask, and no one but Thomas dared reach over and pull it off her head when she was bending down to help Muriel with a math problem. For that, they put him in the cupboard for so long that he tried to claw his way out, his hands bloody and fingernails torn to pieces, trying first to dig holes in the dirt floor and then trying to take apart the thick wooden door, one sliver at a time. He says he'll die before he lets them do that to him again. And that's why my stomach is threatening to throw up the salty oats the closer we get to the cupboard.

"Please don't, Father Jacob, please," I plead, but he's rounded the corner and I can see the tables lined up, the benches pushed under when not in use. I can hear the older kids who do the cooking talking low in the back, but I can't see them. The cupboard door is small and sits under the stairs with an old wooden door and a very firm lock. Father Jacob takes a key from the ring he carries around his waist and unlocks the door just as my stomach betrays me. The oats from that morning, mixed with bile that burns my throat, land on his shoes, dirtying the bottom of his cassock.

"I'm going to add a day for that, Matthew."

He tugs my arm, awkwardly pushing me in through the small opening before closing it. There is the clink of the key and I'm immersed in the dark and the damp. On the other side of the door I hear him yell at the kitchen staff to clean up the mess and bring him some warm water to wash his cassock where I dirtied it. My throat burns and there is sick on my chin. I try to breathe deeply, but it hurts.

It gets quiet in the cupboard, so very quiet. The voices

disappear and the footsteps of Father Jacob fade. I only hear my heart beating, fast and short, and the sound of my shallow breath. The burn subsides in my throat, but the dark persists. It's cold and smells of rotting wood, mould and mice drop-pings. Thomas says rats will eat you alive if you fall asleep. He says that their eyes glow red when they are ready to snack on you. They start with your fingers and toes before moving to your eyes. He says to keep your shoes on and ball your hands into a fist, even when sleeping. That's when they get you. I search the dark for the small red orbs of rats' eyes but see none.

There is nothing to do in the cupboard except imagine. Imagine the rats, the warmth of a fire when you're sitting on cold, packed dirt, the smell of pine and snow when mould is all there is. I imagine the last time I saw my mother. The longer I stay in the dark, the more uncertain I am whether the vision of my mother is a memory or my imagining. She is standing at the edge of the school grounds, where the trees opened and swallowed her. I imagine my sister in her white socks. Socks that she was so proud of, she cried when our mother made her take them off to wash them. I imagine Father Jacob's Christ coming to feed us jam and warm milk. I imagine the others, sitting in class, whispering about me. I imagine the nice to keep the bad away. I imagine until I hear the feet of the others shuffling into the kitchen, pulling out the benches and sitting quietly. Sister Agnus says the prayer and I can feel their eyes, the eyes of those who dare to not bow their head, through the wood of the door. They know I'm here, but they aren't allowed to acknowledge me or the cupboard. Even when it's empty, a glance caught by Sister Agnus will get you a hard slap to the ears.

A click in the lock startles me and I shift to my hands and knees, ready to move into the light again, but a hand stops me. I can see the others at the end of the table, trying not to look at me as Father Jacob pushes me back into the dark.

"You will stay here and read until you're ready to apologize. God and I will know if you make a false apology, so you'd better be ready in your heart and in your head." He hands me the Bible, the one all the kids get when they go to the cupboard. "I have placed holders in places I think you should read and consider. I hope you find guidance in the word of God." The lock clicks and I hear his keys fall into place as he walks away.

The Bible is heavy and the thick leather cover is cracked

in places. I run my fingers along the spine and find a few of the cracks. The paper inside is thin like the skin of an onion. It flutters from an unknown breeze when I open it, the pages flapping and crackling. The only light in the cupboard comes from a crack in the wood door, a thin line of light. Not enough to see out of and barely enough to read by. I'd like to ask for a light, or a candle, but fear of a darker, damper place keeps my lips tight to my teeth. I feel for one of Father Jacob's bookmarks and find one. I have to move the book back and forth, the tiny sliver of light hitting one letter at a time until I can form a whole word. *But Jesus called them unto him, and said, Suffer little children to come unto me, and forbid them not: for of such is the kingdom of God.* So little of this book they make us read makes sense to me.

I don't know how long I am in the cupboard. I know that I sleep, I cry, I pick the dried blood from Sister Agnus's ruler from my hair. I know I am hungry and thirsty, that my mouth still tastes of bile, that I wet myself because I have no choice. The smell of my shame mixes with the mould and the dirt floor. I wait for the rats, my feet tucked under me until my legs go numb with pins and needles and pain, my fingers balled into fists.

I listen to the others as they eat their meals, wondering if they can hear the sound of my hungry belly through the cupboard door. I can hear praying and the scraping of spoons on the metal bowls, the occasional sound of metal hitting the floor and the sisters slapping the child who dared to drop a spoon. No one comes to talk to me, no one comes to check on me. No one brings me food. I begin to memorize all the passages picked out by Father Jacob. I will recite them over and over and over, whispering them into the darkness until I begin to assign meaning to them.

> *Unto thee it was shown, that thou mightest know that the*
> *LORD he is God; there is none else beside him.*
> *—Deuteronomy 4:35*

> *O LORD, there is none like thee, neither is there any God*
> *beside thee, according to all that we have heard with our*
> *ears. —1 Chronicles 17:20*

> *Ye are my witnesses, saith the LORD, and my servant*
> *whom I have chosen: that ye may know and believe me,*
> *and understand that I am he: before me there was no God*

formed, neither shall there be after me. I, even I, am the
LORD; and beside me there is no saviour.
—*Isaiah 43:10, 11*

I like the verses, they're beautiful when they are all you have. I love the way the words match together like a song. The words make the imagining of the good things so much easier. I'm reciting John 17:3, *And this is life eternal, that they might know thee the only true God, and Jesus Christ, whom thou hast sent,* when a small voice seeps through the crack of light. I jump and inhale quickly, coughing.

"What did you do to get sent to the cupboard?" It's my sister's voice through the crack. We barely speak, they don't let us see one another. In winter, it's worse. At least, when the weather is warm, we are allowed to go outside to read, maybe to play games, but most of the time to tend to their garden while they watch. This is when we can talk. Talk, but no hugging or touching. In winter, I see her in passing while we eat, and we smile at one another.

"Go back to your meal. If they find you speaking to me . . ."

"Shhhh. Sister Margarete is keeping watch." We like Sister Margarete as much as we fear Sister Agnus. Sister Margarete has round, red cheeks. The only other thing about her that is round is her laugh. We like to imagine that she has the yellow hair that some white people have and that it is wild with curls under her habit. We imagine that at night, when she takes it off, if she takes it off, her curls leap out and bounce around furiously, glad to be freed. Of course, we don't know what colour her hair is or whether it curls, but the imagination is a powerful medicine in a place like this.

"I asked if God was the same as Kisu'lkw."

My sister sighs on the other side of the door, and I hear her head thud against it just where mine had rested minutes before. "Well, let's pray that they don't keep you in there forever."

We stay quiet, her in the light and me in the dark, until I hear the faint alto of Sister Margarete's voice and the light filters back in through the crack in the door.

My sister's voice is the only one I hear in what I will later learn was four and a half days in the cupboard. When I do emerge, I re-enter the world with all my fingers and toes intact, soiled and sore. The first night I sleep in my bed, my skin burns from the iodine on the open sores, sores I am to blame for since I couldn't control my bladder.

"God's punishment," Father Jacob says as he pours the thick brown liquid on a piece of cotton and dabs at the open wounds. "Now, did you have time to consider the passages that I marked for you?"

I slide my pants up over the abscesses, careful not to graze any.

"And this is life eternal, that they might know thee the only true God, and Jesus Christ, whom thou hast sent," I recite.

"And what does it mean? Why did I want you to consider it?" He watches as I pull on my clean shirt.

"There is only one God, your God, and there are no others."

"*Our* God, Matthew, *our* God. For he loves all his children even when they displease him." He places his hands on my shoulders and bends down, the same way he did the day we arrived. His hands are just as heavy, but I am taller now and he looks awkward, half-bent, but this doesn't seem to bother him. "Now go back to the kitchen and get something to eat."

That day, alone in the kitchen, a bench all to myself, I have oats with jam and warm milk, before I am made to go back to the classroom.

A STRONG SEED

The shimmer from her beaded headpiece, shining in the sun, catches my eye. I squint and look toward the circle. She's waiting, moving her hips back and forth to the music that plays in her head. I can tell my daughter is nervous by the way her lips are pursed and she keeps looking to the sky.

"I'm waiting for the sign she always gives me. Waiting for a sign that everything is going to be good."

I follow her glance and see a pair of red-winged blackbirds flitting above the powwow grounds.

She relaxes her lips and smiles.

This morning, her grandmother braided her hair, the ancient and knotty fingers of my mother expertly weaving hair and ribbon together, the colours so bright against the black. I feel as though I sat there a lifetime ago, my mother pulling at my hair, telling me to stay still. I didn't like the dancing, I still don't. I didn't like people to look at me, to see my feet moving awkwardly in the circle, to see my hand-me-down dress with no beads, to watch as I dropped the feather fan when I wasn't paying enough attention, scrambling to pick it up in time with the drumbeat. I hated the way it was expected of me. I prefer to do my dancing in the kitchen to the songs on the radio. I can hide away, no one judges my clumsiness in my kitchen.

But my girl isn't like me. She doesn't suffer the shyness I was burdened with. She's been waiting for this chance, begging each year to be allowed to dance. Her feet have been dusting the floor of her bedroom night after night, her brother playing the drum for her to practise. Her auntie on her father's side has taught her how to summon the ancestors to the circle.

"You are a strong seed, you are. I will remind you all the time so that you never forget it," my mother told her, ribbon and hair snaking their way through her fingers. "Seeds are planted, and with love and with just the right amount of attention, they grow and become strong. A seed once established will spread its roots to hold them steady. We are your roots, don't forget that. When you feel sad or alone or frightened, remember you are as strong as your roots, and we are the strongest. We still roam these lands and dance these dances and speak our own words. Those, my girl, are strong roots that will make a strong seed that will, in time, sprout a beautiful woman. You are a strong seed, you are." She finished off the braid, tied the ribbons together at the end and patted my daughter on the shoulder. Standing, her back stiff, she bent slightly to kiss my daughter on the top of the head. "A strong seed," she whispered again, before disappearing in search of a cup of tea.

"A strong seed," she whispered, watching her grandmother disappear into the kitchen, running her hands over the smooth hair and down each braid.

Now she stands in the circle, waiting, watching the older girls. Her dress sways from side to side as she moves her hips, just starting to expand. This makes her father nervous, and I like to tease him.

"See her there, swaying to the music in her head? She's confident, that daughter of yours. And every day becoming more of a woman."

He glances over at her, the smile deepening before he grunts and moves off to find our younger daughter, the one who still calls him Daddy and looks at him with the childish affection he craves from his girls. I laugh as he walks away, and my mother swats me.

"Leave him be. It's hard for a man to watch his little girls grow into women," she scolds.

I look back to the circle. The other girls are starting to assemble, their beads glowing in the sunlight. Her cousin stands next to her, chatting as the drummers take their seats, drinking their water and preparing themselves. She's watched these girls for thirteen years, standing on the sidelines. She would sway, her hands in the air, moving her tiny bare feet with them. Today she lifts the feather fan her father made her toward the sun.

MY DAUGHTER SEWED the dress herself, under the watchful eye of her grandmother. She picked out the colours for her dress, red, black and yellow. She's a soft girl, delicate but not shy; the quiet colours suit her well. Her auntie helped her with the beadwork, but again she insisted on designing her own—a red-winged blackbird in flight, a beaded sun behind it. And as strong as she is and becomes, she is also stubborn, a trait I am told comes from me.

I run down the hall at the sound of her yelling.

"I can't do this! It's too hard!" She sucks on the end of her finger, a small dot of blood on the tip, the needle hanging from the beaded leather.

"You can do this, don't be so foolish. Just be patient and a little more careful. And no more yelling. You scared me near to death." I close her bedroom door but leave it open a crack until I see her start back at it again, the black body and red wings of a bird taking shape. "And it wouldn't hurt you to ask for help once in a while."

"I can do it," she says just loud enough for me to hear as I reach the kitchen. "I want to do it."

Her father bought her a pair of summer moccasins, had them made to match her regalia, but she insisted on the leather boots. The ones with red beading, the same ones I wore when I danced, the first and the last time. The intricate flowers intertwined with the swirly green beaded vines. They had been stored in a closet now for years, behind the winter jackets and miscellaneous mittens without a match but bound up in the silly hope that the mate would be found someday. The boots were creased where they had been folded and the white rabbit fur was tamped down, flat from being stored away for so long. I still don't know how she found them, and she refuses to tell me, although I have the feeling my mother may have had something to do with it.

"Your great-grandfather, one of the last of us to live off the land, killed a moose when I was just young like you," my mother told her, holding the boots in the air, inspecting them, revering them. "He used the leather to make each of his family something special to keep the spirit of the animal alive. These were mine and then your mother's. These boots are a root, you remember that. A strong root."

In the field, the drum starts. The beat is powerful, and I can feel it in my belly. It reminds me of when I carried her, her tiny feet pressing against my stretched skin. When she was small, I told her that she had been a dancer even before she came into the world. The singers start, their voices echoing off the sky, and the women begin to move. She stands there for just a moment and then sticks her foot out, her toes touching first, one hand on her hip, the other carrying the feathered fan, the ribbons that hold it together bouncing with her. The soft leather of her boots is shaded dark by the wet grass, the result of an early morning shower.

She is slow to start, eyeing the others. Her cousin, dancing in the circle beside her, gives her a wink, and she smiles and begins to move with the rhythm of the drum. My mother, seated beside me, takes my hand in hers, her skin soft and wrinkled. I stand beside her, watching, holding her hand, trying not to cry. She is beautiful, this dancer of mine.

"I believe we've planted a good one," I say to my mother.

"Taho!" she replies.

ACKNOWLEDGEMENTS

As you may have seen in the dedication, these are not all my stories. These stories belong to so many people. Some of them I have met, most I haven't, but in my forty-seven years I have come across a piece of their story and my imagination took hold. And some of these stories are purely from my imagination.

Specifically, I want to thank my grandmother, Doris Peters, who may not be with us anymore but once told me a story about a tree where women used to give birth. Thank you to Jessie Hemphill, who put the story "Ashes" in my mind, and to Rye Barberstock for "A Strong Seed." To my aunt Lorraine Whitman, who gifted me the story of how the crow became black.

To my agent, Marilyn Biderman, you have worked miracles for me, and I am forever grateful. To my editor Janice Zawerbny at HarperCollins Canada, thank you for your gentle touch and consistent encouragement. Thank you for helping me make these stories the best versions of themselves. And to everyone at HarperCollins Canada, thank you.

Thank you to friends Christy Ann Conlin and Nathan Sack, who read these when they were young and new and gave me the confidence to continue with them, to write more, to edit and add. Wela'lioq.

To my mentor and friend katherena vermette, who spent hours on the phone in Winnipeg, walking her dogs while I paced across my living room in Nova Scotia. Those calls helped me to mould these stories, helped me become a better storyteller. Wela'lin, nitape'skw.

And finally, to my family, thank you for your constant encouragement and support. I feel truly lucky to have you as my family. My mom, Juanita, my dad, Larry, my stepmom, Terry. To my siblings and their partners, Courtney, Catherine and James, Michael and Audrey, Taylor and Judd. To my nieces and nephews, who are some of my very favourite people on earth, Sierra, Oliver, Paisley, Waylon, Greyson, Colton and

Riley (don't worry, no more socks for Christmas) and Baby Faye. To Erica, Tyler and Bradley, my almost siblings. And to Shannon, my best friend—thanks for putting up with me for the last three and a half decades.

I wrote this collection before I wrote *The Berry Pickers*, so I often like to call these stories my writing training wheels. If you happen to stumble upon them, I hope you enjoy.

AMANDA PETERS is a writer of Mi'kmaq and settler ancestry. Her debut novel, *The Berry Pickers*, was the winner of the Andrew Carnegie Medal for Excellence in Fiction and the 2023 Barnes & Noble Discover Prize, and was a finalist for the Atwood Gibson Writers' Trust Fiction Prize and the Amazon.ca First Novel Award. Her work has also appeared in *The Antigonish Review, Grain, Alaska Quarterly Review, The Dalhousie Review*, and *filling Station*. She is the winner of the 2021 Indigenous Voices Award for Unpublished Prose and a participant in the 2021 Writers' Trust Rising Stars program. Peters is a graduate of the MFA program at the Institute of American Indian Arts in Santa Fe, New Mexico, and has a certificate in creative writing from the University of Toronto. She lives and writes in the Annapolis Valley, Nova Scotia, where she teaches English and creative writing at Acadia University.